Agatha Raisin AND THE

WELLSPRING ~ OF ~ DEATH

The Agatha Raisin series
(listed in order)

Agatha Raisin
AND THE
WELLSPRING OF DEATH

M. C. Beaton

ROBINSON

Constable & Robinson Ltd
3 The Lanchesters
162 Fulham Palace Road
London W6 9ER

www.constablerobinson.com

First published in the USA 1998 by St Martin's Press
175 Fifth Avenue, New York, NY 10010

This edition published by Robinson,
an imprint of Constable & Robinson Ltd 2010

ISBN: 978-1-84901-140-2

Printed and bound by
CPI Group (UK) Ltd, Croydon, CR0 4YY

5 7 9 10 8 6 4

AGATHA RAISIN

Agatha Raisin was born in a tower block slum in Birmingham and christened Agatha Styles. No middle names. Agatha had often longed for at least two middle names such as Caroline or Olivia. Her parents, Joseph and Margaret Styles, were both unemployed and both drunks. They lived on benefits and the occasional bout of shoplifting.

Agatha attended the local comprehensive as a rather shy and sensitive child but quickly developed a bullying, aggressive manner so that the other pupils would steer clear of her.

At the age of fifteen, her parents decided it was time she earned her keep and her mother found her work in a biscuit factory, checking packets of biscuits on a conveyer belt for any faults.

As soon as Agatha had squirreled away enough money, she ran off to London and found work as a waitress and studied computing at evening classes. But she fell in love with a customer at the restaurant, Jimmy Raisin. Jimmy had curly black hair and bright blue eyes and a great deal of charm. He seemed to have plenty of money to throw around. He wanted an affair, but besotted as she was, Agatha held out for marriage.

They moved into one room in a lodging house in Finsbury Park where Jimmy's money soon ran out (he would never say where it came from in the first place). And he drank. Agatha found she had escaped the frying pan into the fire.

She was fiercely ambitious. One night, when she came home and found Jimmy stretched out on the bed dead drunk, she packed her things and escaped.

She found work as a secretary at a public relations firm and soon moved into doing public relations herself. Her mixture of bullying and cajoling brought her success. She saved and saved until she could start her own business.

But Agatha had always been a dreamer. Years back when she had been a child her parents had taken her on one glorious holiday. They had rented a cottage in the Cotswolds for a week. Agatha never forgot that golden holiday or the beauty of the countryside.

So as soon as she had amassed a great deal of money, she took early retirement and bought a cottage in the village of Carsely in the Cotswolds.

Her first attempt at detective work came after she cheated at a village quiche baking competition by putting a shop bought quiche in as her own. The judge died of poisoning and shamed Agatha had to find the real killer. Her adventures there are covered in the first Agatha Raisin mystery, *The Quiche of Death*, and in the series of novels that follow. As successful as she is in detecting, she constantly remains unlucky in love. Will she ever find happiness with the man of her dreams? Watch this space!

Chapter One

Agatha Raisin was bored and unhappy. Her neighbour, James Lacey, had returned at last to the cottage next door to her own in the Cotswold village of Carsely. She tried to tell herself that she was no longer in love with him and that his coldness towards her did not matter.

She had almost married him, but her husband, still then very much alive, had surfaced at the wedding ceremony, and James had never really forgiven her for her deception.

One spring evening when the village was ablaze with daffodils, forsythia, magnolia and crocuses, Agatha trudged along to the vicarage to a meeting of the Carsely Ladies' Society, hoping to find some gossip to enliven the tedium of her days.

But such that there was did not interest her because it concerned a spring of water in the neighbouring village of Ancombe.

1

Agatha knew the spring. In the eighteenth century, a Miss Jakes had channelled the spring through the bottom of her garden, through a pipe in the garden wall, and into a fountain for the use of the public. The water gushed out through the mouth of a skull – a folly which had caused no end of criticism even in the grim days of the eighteenth century – then to a shallow basin sunk into the ground, over the lip of the basin and down through a grating and under the road. On the other side, it became a little stream which meandered through other gardens until it joined the river Ancombe.

Some lines of doggerel, penned by Miss Jakes, had been engraved above the skull. They read:

Weary traveller, stop and stare
At the water gushing here.
We live our days in this Vale of Strife.
Bend and drink deep of the Waters of Life.

Two hundred years ago, the water was held to have magical, restorative properties, but now only walkers paused to fill their flasks, and occasionally locals like Agatha brought along a bottle to fill up and take home to make tea, the water being softer than the stuff which came out of the tap.

Recently, the newly formed Ancombe Water

Company had attempted to secure permission from the Ancombe Parish Council to drain water from the spring each day, paying a penny a gallon.

'Many are saying it is sacrilege,' said Mrs Bloxby, the vicar's wife. 'But there was never anything religious about the spring.'

'It is bringing a sour note of commercialism into our gentle rural life,' protested a new-comer to the ladies' society, a Mrs Darry, who had recently moved to the Cotswolds from London and had all the incomer's zeal for preserving village life.

'I say it won't bother anyone,' said the secretary, Miss Simms, crossing her black-stockinged legs and showing with a flash of thigh that they were the hold-up variety. 'I mean ter say, the truck for the water's going to come each day at dawn. After that, anyone can help themselves as usual.'

Agatha stifled a yawn. As a retired business-woman who had run her own successful public relations company, she thought it was a sound commercial idea.

She did not like Mrs Darry, who had a face like a startled ferret, so she said, 'The Cotswolds are highly commercialized already, bursting with bus tours and tea-shops and craft-shops.'

The room then split up into three factions, those for the business plan, those against, and those like Agatha who were heartily bored with the whole thing.

Mrs Bloxby took Agatha aside as she was leaving, her gentle face concerned.

'You are looking a bit down in the dumps, Agatha,' she said. 'Is it James?'

'No,' lied Agatha defensively. 'It's the time of year. It always gets me down.'

'"April is the cruellest month."'

Agatha blinked rapidly. She suspected a literary quotation and she hated quotations, damning them as belonging to some arty-farty world.

'Just so,' she grumped and made her way out into the sweet evening air.

A magnolia tree glistened waxily in the silence of the vicarage garden. Over in the churchyard daffodils, bleached white by moonlight, nestled up to old leaning tombstones.

I must buy a plot in the churchyard, thought Agatha. How comforting to rest one's last under that blanket of shaggy grass and flowers. She sighed. Life at that moment was just a bowl of withered fruit, with a stone in every one.

She had almost forgotten about the water company. But a week later Roy Silver phoned her. Roy had been her employee when she had run her own business and now worked for the company which had bought her out. He was in a high state of excitement.

'Listen to this, Aggie,' he chirped. 'That Ancombe Water Company – heard of it?'

'Yes.'

'They're our new clients and as their office is in Mircester, the boss wondered if you would like to handle the account on a freelance basis.'

Agatha looked steelily at the phone. Roy Silver was the one who had found her husband so that he had turned up just as she was about to get married to James.

'No,' she said curtly and replaced the phone.

She sat looking at it for a few minutes and then, plucking up courage, picked up the receiver and dialled James's number.

He answered after the first ring. 'James,' said Agatha with an awful false brightness. 'What about dinner tonight?'

'I am very sorry,' he said crisply. 'I am busy. And,' he went on quickly, as if to forestall any further invitation, 'I shall be busy for the next few weeks.'

Agatha very gently replaced the receiver. Her stomach hurt. People always talked about hearts breaking but the pain was always right in the gut.

A blackbird sang happily somewhere in the garden, the sweetness of the song intensifying the pain inside Agatha.

She picked up the phone again and dialled the number of Mircester police headquarters and asked to speak to her friend, Detective Sergeant Bill Wong, and, having been told it was his day off, phoned him at home.

'Agatha,' said Bill, pleased. 'I'm not doing anything today. Why don't you come over?'

Agatha hesitated. She found Bill's parents rather grim. 'I'm afraid it will just be me,' went on Bill. 'Ma and Pa have gone to Southend to see some relatives.'

'I'll be over,' said Agatha.

She drove off, eyes averted from James's cottage.

Bill was delighted to see her. He was in his twenties, with a round face and a figure newly trimmed down.

'You're looking fit, Bill,' said Agatha. 'New girlfriend?' Bill's love life could be assessed from his figure, which quickly became plump the minute there was no romance in the offing.

'Yes. Her name is Sharon. She's a typist at the station. Very pretty.'

'Introduced her yet to your mother and father?'

'Not yet.'

So he would be all right for a while, thought Agatha cynically. Bill adored his parents and could never understand why the minute he introduced one of his lady-loves to them, the romance was immediately over.

'I was just about to have lunch,' said Bill.

'I'll take you somewhere. My treat,' said Agatha quickly. Bill's cooking was as awful as that of his mother.

'All right. There's quite a good pub at the end of the road.'

The pub, called the Jolly Red Cow, was a dismal place, dominated by a pool table where the unemployed, white-faced youth of Mircester passed their daylight hours.

Agatha ordered chicken salad. The lettuce was limp and the chicken stringy. Bill tucked into a greasy egg, sausage and chips with every appearance of enjoyment.

'So what's new, Bill? Anything exciting?'

'Nothing much. Things have been quite quiet, thank goodness. What about you? Seen much of James?'

Agatha's face went stiff. 'No, I haven't seen much of him. That's over. I don't want to talk about it.'

Bill said hurriedly, as if anxious to change the subject, 'What's all this fuss about the new water company?'

'Oh, that. They were talking about it at the ladies' society last week. I can't get excited about it. I mean, I don't see what the fuss is about. They're coming at dawn each day to take off the water and for the rest of the day everything will be as normal.'

'I've got a nasty feeling in my bones about this,' said Bill, dousing his chips with ketchup. 'Anything to do with the environment, and sooner or later some protest group is going to turn up, and sooner or later there's going to be violence.'

'I shouldn't think so.' Agatha poked disconsolately at a piece of chicken. 'Ancombe's a pretty dead sort of place.'

'You might be surprised. Even in dead-alive sort of places there can be a rumpus. There are militant groups who don't care about the environment at all. All they want is an excuse for a punch-up. I sometimes think they're in the majority. The people who really care about some feature of the environment are usually a small, dedicated group who set out on a peaceful protest, and before they know where they are, they find themselves joined by the militants, and often some of them can end up getting badly hurt.'

'It doesn't interest me,' said Agatha. 'In fact, to be honest, nothing much interests me these days.'

He looked at her in affectionate concern. 'What you want is for me to produce a murder for you to investigate. Well, I'm not going to do it. You can't go around expecting people to be murdered just to provide you with a hobby.'

'It's a bit rude calling it a hobby. What *is* this crap?' She pushed her plate angrily away.

'I think the food here is very good,' said Bill defensively 'You're just being picky because you're unhappy.'

'I'm slimming anyway. The wretched Roy Silver phoned me up wanting me to do public relations for this water company.'

'There's a thing. Their office is right here in Mircester.'

'I'm retired.'

'And unhappy and miserable. Why don't you take it on?'

But Agatha was not going to tell him the real reason for her refusal. Days away at the office meant days away from James Lacey, who might miraculously soften towards her.

After they had parted, Bill went thoughtfully home. On impulse, he phoned James.

'How are things going?' asked James cheerfully. 'I haven't seen you in ages.'

'You've been abroad. I've just been having lunch with Agatha and realized I hadn't spoken to you for some time.'

'Oh.' And James's 'oh' was so frigid that Bill thought if he were holding some cartoon phone receiver there would be icicles forming down the wire. So he chatted idly about this and that while all the while he wanted to ask James why he did not give poor Agatha a break and take her out for dinner.

* * *

A week later Agatha had just finished her usual breakfast of four cigarettes and three strong cups of black coffee when the phone rang. 'Let it be James,' she pleaded to that anthropomorphic God with the long beard and shaggy hair with whom she often, in moments of stress, did deals. 'Let it be James and I'll never smoke again.'

But the God of Agatha's understanding owed more to mythology than anything else and so she was hardly surprised to find out it was Roy Silver on the other end of the line.

'Don't hang up,' said Roy quickly. 'Look, you've still got a grudge against me because I found your husband.'

'And ruined my life,' said Agatha bitterly.

'Well, he's dead now, isn't he? And if James doesn't want to marry you, that's hardly my fault.'

Agatha hung up.

The doorbell went. Perhaps He had heard her prayer. She stubbed out her cigarette.

'Last one,' she said loudly to the ceiling.

She opened the door.

Mrs Darry stood there.

'I wondered if you would do me a favour, Mrs Raisin.'

'Come in,' said Agatha bleakly. She led the way into the kitchen, sat down at the table, and gloomily lit a cigarette.

Mrs Darry sat down. 'I would be grateful if you refrained from smoking.'

'Tough,' said Agatha. 'This is my house and my cigarette. What do you want?'

'Don't you know you are killing yourself?'

Agatha looked at her cigarette and then at Mrs Darry. 'As long as I am killing myself, I am not killing you. Out with it. What do you want?'

'Water.'

'There's water in the tap. Has yours been cut off?'

'No, you do not understand. My mother is coming to stay.'

Agatha blinked. Mrs Darry she judged to be in her late sixties.

'Mother is ninety-two,' went on Mrs Darry. 'She is very partial to good tea. I do not have a car and I wondered whether you would get me a flask of water from the spring at Ancombe?'

'I did not intend to go to Ancombe,' said Agatha, thinking how much she disliked this newcomer to the village. She was such an ugly woman. How odd that people could be so ugly, not particularly because of appearance, but because of the atmosphere of judgemental bad temper and discontent they carried around with them.

She was wearing one of those sleeveless quilted jackets, tightly buttoned up over a high-necked blouse. Her pointed nose, her pursed mouth and her sandy hair and her pale green hunting eyes made her look more than ever to Agatha like some vicious feral animal, always looking for the kill.

'Is there no one else you could ask?' Agatha considered offering Mrs Darry coffee, and then decided against it.

'Everyone else is so busy,' mourned Mrs Darry. 'I mean, it's not as if you have much to do.'

'As a matter of fact I do,' retorted Agatha, stung to the quick. 'I am going to be handling the public relations for the new water company.'

Mrs Darry gathered up her handbag and gloves and got to her feet. 'I am surprised at you, Mrs Raisin. That you who live in this village should be aiding and abetting a company that is out to destroy our environment is beyond belief.'

'Push off,' said Agatha.

Left alone, she lit another cigarette. On and off during that day, she turned over in her mind the idea of representing the water company. Of course, the offer might not still be open. If she was employed in the launch, then she would need to work very hard, and if she was working very hard, she would not be impelled to make any more silly phone calls to James and suffer the inevitable rejection.

A poor evening on television did little to lighten her mood. She ate a whole bar of chocolate and felt the waistline of her skirt tighten alarmingly. In vain did she tell herself that the constricting feeling at her middle was probably psychosomatic. She decided on impulse to take a flask and walk over to Ancombe and get some water for tea, and to take another look at the spring.

It was another beautiful evening. Bird cherry starred the hedgerows, orchards on either side of the road glimmered with apple blossom. She trudged along, a stocky figure, feeling diminished by the glory of the night.

The walk to Ancombe was several miles and by the time she approached the spring, she was weary and already regretting her decision not to take the car.

The spring was at the far end of the village, the unlit end, where the houses stopped and the countryside began again.

As she approached she could hear the tinkling sound of the water.

She was about to bend over the spring when she started back with a gasp of alarm and dropped her flask. For lying at her feet, staring up at the faint light from the moon and stars above, was a dead man.

Very dead, thought Agatha, feeling for his pulse and finding none.

She ran back to the nearest house, roused the occupants and phoned the police.

Waving aside offers of brandy or tea, Agatha returned resolutely to the spring and waited. Word quickly spread around the village and by the time the police arrived, there was a silent circle of people around the body. The skull above the spring glared maliciously at them from over the dead man's body.

Agatha learned from the hushed whispers that the body was that of a Mr Robert Struthers, chairman of Ancombe Parish Council. Blood was seeping from the back of his head into the spring, blood, black in the night, swirling around the stone basin.

Sirens tore through the silence of the night. The police had arrived at last. Bill would not be among them. It was his day off.

But Agatha recognized Detective Inspector Wilkes.

She sat in one of the police cars and made a statement to a policewoman. She felt quite numb. She was told to wait and a police car would take her home.

At last she was dropped off at her own cottage. She hesitated on her doorstep, looking wistfully towards the cottage next door. Here was a splendid opportunity to talk to James. But the shock of finding the dead man had changed something in her. I'm worth better than that, thought Agatha, as she unlocked her door and went in.

She was just making herself a cup of coffee when the doorbell rang. This time she did not expect to see James standing on the doorstep and it was with genuine gratitude and relief that she welcomed the vicar's wife, Mrs Bloxby.

'I heard the terrible news,' said Mrs Bloxby, pushing a strand of grey hair behind her ear. 'I came along to spend the night with you. You won't want to be alone.'

Agatha looked at her with affection, remembering nights before when Mrs Bloxby had volunteered to keep her company. 'I think I'll be all right,' she said, 'but I'd be grateful if you would stay for a bit.'

Mrs Bloxby followed her into the kitchen and sat down. 'Mrs Darry phoned me with the news. If you look out, you'll see lights all over the village. They'll be talking about it all night.'

'Tell me about this water business,' said Agatha, handing her a mug of coffee. 'I assume they were asked to make a decision on the water.'

'Yes, indeed, and some very noisy debates they had on the subject, too.'

'Who owns the water?'

'Well, it comes from Mrs Toynbee's garden, but as the well is out on the road, that bit belongs to the parish. There are seven members of the parish council and they've all served for years.'

'What about council elections?'

'Oh, those come and go but nobody else wanted the job and so nobody ever stands against them. The late Mr Struthers was chairman, Mr Andy Stiggs is vice chairman, and the rest – Miss Mary Owen, Mrs Jane Cutler, Mr Bill Allen, Mr Fred Shaw, and Miss Angela Buckley. Mr Struthers was a retired banker. Mr Stiggs is a retired shopkeeper, Miss Mary Owen, independently wealthy. Mrs Jane Cutler, also wealthy, is a widow, Mr Bill Allen runs the garden centre, Mr Fred Shaw is the local electrician and Miss Angela Buckley is a farmer's daughter.'

'And who was for selling the water and who against?'

'As far as I remember, Mrs Cutler, Fred Shaw and Angela Buckley were for it, and Mary Owen, Bill Allen and Andy Stiggs, against. The chairman had the casting vote and as far as I know he had not yet made up his mind.'

'It could be that one of the fors or one of the againsts could have known which way he was going to vote and didn't like it,' said Agatha, her bearlike eyes gleaming under the heavy fringe of her brown hair.

'I shouldn't really think so. They are all quite

elderly, except Miss Buckley, who is in her forties. They have all led unblemished lives.'

'But this seems to have stirred them all up.'

'Yes,' said Mrs Bloxby reluctantly. 'The debates have been hot and furious. And of course the villagers themselves are split into two camps. Mary Owen claims the villagers have not been consulted and she is holding a meeting in the village hall. I think it was due to take place next week but I am sure it will be put off in view of this murder.'

'If it does turn out to be murder,' said Agatha slowly. 'I mean, he was old and he was lying face-up. He could have had a seizure, fallen backwards and struck his head on the basin.'

'Let's hope that is the case. If not, the press will arrive and television crews will arrive and it is so beautiful here that we will have to suffer from more tourists than usual.'

'I'm a bit of a tourist myself,' said Agatha huffily. 'I don't really belong here. It drives me mad when people in the village complain about those terrible tourists when they've just come back from a holiday abroad where they've been tourists themselves.'

'That's not quite true,' said the vicar's wife gently. 'Carsely people do not like leaving Carsely.'

'I don't care. They go into Evesham and Moreton to do their shopping, so they are taking up someone else's bit of space. The world is one planet full of tourists.'

'Or displaced people. Think of Bosnia.'

'Bugger Bosnia,' said Agatha with all the venom of one who has been made to feel guilty. 'Sorry,' she mumbled. 'I must be a bit upset.'

'I am sure you are. It must have been a shocking experience.'

And it had been, thought Agatha. Some women such as herself were cursed with the same machismo as men. Her first thought had been to say, 'Oh, it was all right. I'm used to dead bodies, you know.' But Agatha had been afraid of so many things during her life that she had gone through the world with her fists swinging until the gentle life of Carsely and the kindness of the villagers had got under the carapace she had created for herself.

'If it should be murder and I concentrate on that,' said Agatha slowly, 'I might take this job of public relations officer for the Ancombe Water Company.'

'Mrs Darry said you already had it.'

'What a gossip that frump is! I only told her because she called round to ask me to get her some water from the spring and said, more or less, that I had nothing else to do. She made me feel as if I were already on the scrap-heap.'

'It could be dangerous for you if you asked too many questions.'

'If it's murder, it will probably be quickly solved. One of the fors didn't want Struthers to block it or one of the againsts thought he was going to break up village life and pollute the environment.'

'I don't think that can be the case. You don't know the parish council; I do. Certainly this issue has made them very heated, but they are stable, ordinary members of the community. Shall you and James be investigating it? You have both had a lot of success in the past.'

'He has been very rude to me and snubbed me,' said Agatha. 'No, I shall not go near him.'

When Mrs Bloxby left, Agatha got ready for bed. The old cottage creaked as it usually did when it settled down for the night and various wildlife rustled in the thatch. But every little noise made her jump and she wished she had not pretended to be so brave and had asked the vicar's wife to stay the night. Then there was James, just next door, who must have heard of the murder by now. He should be here with her to protect and comfort her. A tear rolled down Agatha's nose and she fell into an uneasy sleep.

Another fine spring day did much to banish the horrors of the night before, and Bill Wong called, accompanied by a policewoman, to go over her statement.

James Lacey had seen the police car arrive, knew all about the murder and that it was Agatha who had found the body. He had assumed she would call him, for he was eager for details, but finally Bill Wong left and his phone did not ring.

Agatha phoned Roy Silver. 'I've decided to take that freelance job with the water company,' she said gruffly. Roy longed for the power to tell her to get lost, but the fact that his boss would look on the getting of Agatha as a great coup stopped him.

'Great,' he said coldly. 'I'll set up a meeting for you tomorrow with the directors.'

'I suppose you've seen the papers?' said Agatha.

'What about?'

'The chairman of Ancombe Parish Council was found dead last night – by me.'

'Never! You're quite a little vulture, Aggie. They'll need you more than ever to counteract the bad publicity. Is it murder?'

'Could be, but he was very old and maybe just fell over and struck his head on the stone basin.'

'Anyway, I'll get back to you, sweetie, and give you the time you're to see them.'

'Who will I be dealing with?'

'Co-directors, Guy and Peter Freemont, brothers.'

'What's their pedigree?'

'City businessmen, wheeler-dealers, you know the kind.'

'All right, let me know.'

Agatha looked at the clock. Nearly lunchtime. She decided to go along to the Red Lion, the local pub, and see what gossip she could glean. Perhaps James might be there . . . forget it!

She made up with care, studying her face intently in her fright mirror, one of those magnifying ones. Her skin was still smooth on her cheeks but there were threads of wrinkles about her eyes and nasty ones on her upper lip. Her hair was thick and glossy and her legs were good. Her figure was a bit on the stocky side and her neck was a trifle short. She sighed as she spread foundation cream over the wrinkles and then applied powder and lipstick. She reached for a tube of mascara and then decided against it. Waterproof mascara simply meant it took longer to clean off and had a habit of sticking under her eyes for days. She should get her eyelashes dyed. Would a face-lift be worth it, or would it stop her from facing up to ageing gracefully? Did anyone ever age gracefully, or was it a choice between giving up or going down fighting?

As she walked along to the pub, she was assailed with a feeling of loneliness, of isolation, and wondered, not for the first time, if the city was so deep in her bones that she could never put down roots in country soil. And yet it was all so beautiful and calm as she walked under arches of blossom. Far above her, the Cotswold sky was pale blue and cloudless. Going to be another hose-pipe ban soon, thought the practical side of Agatha.

She was nearly at the pub when she realized she had forgotten to feed her two cats, Hodge and Boswell. She groaned. They would be all right until she got back. She was not going to turn into one of those drivelling women who were sentimental about animals.

Nevertheless, she walked back to her cottage, fed her cats, let them out in the garden, and feeling she had endured enough exercise and fresh air for one day, got into her car and drove the short distance to the pub, plunging happily into its beer-smelling, smoky gloom.

The barman, John Fletcher, gave her a gin and tonic and then the locals clustered around, anxious for news. Always happy to be the centre of attention, Agatha described in gruesome detail the finding of the body. 'It may not be murder,' she finished. 'He could just have fallen.'

'Bound to be murder,' said Miss Simms, secretary of the Carsely Ladies' Society and the village's best-known unmarried mother. 'And I know who done it!'

'Who?' asked Agatha.

Miss Simms cradled her half-pint of beer against her chest. 'It was that Mary Owen.'

'Go on with you,' said Fred Griggs, the local policeman, lumbering up to join the group. 'Mary Owen is a nice old lady who wouldn't hurt a fly.'

'How old?' asked Agatha.

'Sixty-five.'

Agatha winced. She was in her middle fifties and did not like to think of anyone in their sixties being considered old.

'She may have been nice one time,' said Miss Simms defiantly, 'but ever since this water company's come on the scene, she's been hollering and yelling about it. People can go batty when they get as old as that.'

'We don't know yet it was murder,' said Fred. 'Is anyone going to buy me a drink?'

'I will,' said Agatha. 'Drinking on duty?'

'Day off. I'll have a pint of Hook Norton.'

'I didn't think you could get a day off with there being this death.'

'The detectives are handling it.'

Mrs Darry came up and joined them. Agatha turned her back on her, trying to exclude her from the group, but Mrs Darry pushed past her.

'Are you talking about the murder?' she asked eagerly.

'We have other things to talk about,' said Agatha huffily as she paid for the policeman's drink.

'I was saying as how Mary Owen did it,' said Miss Simms.

'I'm surprised to find you here, Mrs Raisin,' said Mrs Darry. 'I'll have a Dubonnet, John.' She looked at Agatha. 'I mean, I thought they would have been grilling you at police headquarters.'

'Why?' Agatha stared at her belligerently.

Mrs Darry gave a malicious little titter. 'Surely the person who is found with the body is always chief suspect?'

'That's rubbish,' said Fred. 'Mrs Raisin just happened to come across the body.'

'It's amazing how many bodies Mrs Raisin seems to have come across.' Mrs Darry took a birdlike sip of her drink. 'And gained a certain notoriety for it, too. Life has been quite quiet for you recently, has it not?'

Agatha's face flamed red with anger. 'Are you saying I go around murdering people so as to get in the newspapers?'

Mrs Darry gave a shrill laugh. 'Just my little joke.'

'Then you can take your joke and shove it up your scrawny arse,' raged Agatha, as the whole full force of the shock of finding the body hit her. Her eyes filled with tears.

'Come on, now,' said Miss Simms, unhitching herself from the bar-stool. 'We'll find a quiet corner away from this bitch.'

Agatha sat down with her, her knees trembling.

'Sorry about the scene,' she mumbled. 'I did get a bit of a fright.'

'Have the press been bothering you?'

'No,' said Agatha, surprised. 'I wonder why.'

'All it said in the *Gloucester Echo* was that the body had been found by a local woman.'

Despite her distress, Agatha felt peeved. The police could have said something like, 'The body was found by Mrs Agatha Raisin, who has been of great help to us in solving murders in the past.'

'That Mrs Darry is an awful cat,' said Miss Simms.

'There's one in every village,' said Agatha gloomily. 'I shouldn't have risen to her remarks.'

'Look, Mrs Raisin . . .'

'Call me Agatha. Why is it we always seem to call each other by our second names?'

'I like that,' said Miss Simms. 'More genteel, like. Are you going to investigate? Will Mr Lacey be helping you?'

'I don't know what James is doing these days and I don't care,' said Agatha. 'But I will probably find out more about the whole set-up because I will be doing public relations for the new water company on a freelance basis.'

'Pity it's water,' said Miss Simms. 'Now if it was gin or whisky, you could get us all some free samples. My current boyfriend is in bathroom equipment. I can get you a toilet seat.'

'That's kind of you, but my toilet seats are all right. Do you know any of the members of the parish council?'

'Ancombe, you mean. The ladies' society did a concert over in Ancombe when you was away abroad. Old fuddy-duddies. Wouldn't hurt a fly. Probably it'll turn out the old geezer just fell over.'

The conversation moved to village gossip and Agatha finally left, feeling better. There was a message on her answering machine from Roy. She was to meet the two directors of the Ancombe Water Company the following day at three in the afternoon.

Comforted by the thought of work, and by a long walk in the afternoon, Agatha managed at last to get a good night's sleep.

Chapter Two

Misery had its compensations. Agatha found she could get into a tailored skirt which had been too tight at the waist when she had last tried it on a few months ago. She also put on a shirt blouse and tailored jacket, packed a writing-pad and pens into a Gucci briefcase, and decided she was ready for her new job.

One of the pleasures of being independently wealthy, she thought, was she did not care very much whether she got the job or not.

She stopped on her way out of the village at the general store and bought the newspapers. Nothing much yet. Only small paragraphs in each to say the police were continuing their investigations into the death of Mr Struthers.

She drove to Mircester and then through the main town and out to an industrial estate on the fringe where the new water company was situated.

Her practised eye took in the sparse furnishings of the entrance hall. Low sofa, table, glossy magazines, green plants in pots. Good appearance but not that much money spent.

The receptionist with a smooth brown skin and large doe-like eyes had a Jamaican accent and shoulder-pads like an American football player. She took Agatha's name, rang someone and then said, 'The secretary will be with you presently.'

Now let's see how long they keep me waiting, thought Agatha. Successful company directors did not play at being important.

After two minutes a tall, willowy Princess Di look-alike swanned in. 'Mrs Raisin? Follow me, if you please.' Following a waft of Givenchy's Amarige, Agatha trailed behind the vision along a corridor of offices. There didn't seem to be much sound coming from behind those office doors. Agatha wondered if they were empty.

The secretary opened a door at the end of the corridor marked 'Boardroom' and stood aside to let Agatha enter.

Agatha cast a quick eye around the boardroom. Long oak table, six chairs, venetian blinds at the two windows, table in the corner with coffee machine, cups, milk, sugar and biscuits.

'If you will sit here, Mrs Raisin.' The secretary drew out a chair at the end of the table. 'Coffee?'

'Black, please, and an ashtray.'

'I don't think we have an ashtray.'

'If I am going to work for you, you'd better find one,' said Agatha, made tetchy with all the guilt the smoker feels these days.

The secretary had wide blue eyes fringed with black lashes. A little flicker of dislike flashed in the blue shallows of her eyes and then was immediately gone.

'What's your name?' asked Agatha.

'Portia Salmond.'

'Well, Portia, are we going to get down to business this day?'

'Mr Peter and Mr Guy will be with you directly.' Portia went to the coffee machine and poured a cup of coffee for Agatha. She returned and put it down in front of her, along with an extra saucer. 'You can use that until I manage to find an ashtray.'

The door at the far end of the room opened and a man entered, hand outstretched.

'I am Peter Freemont,' he said. 'Guy will be along in a minute.'

Peter Freemont was about forty years old, powerful and swarthy with black hair already greying at the temples. He had a large fleshy nose and a small mouth, thick bushy eyebrows and a very large head. His broad figure was encased in a pin-striped suit and his feet, which were tiny, in black lace-up shoes, like children's shoes. He looked like the figure of a man painted on the side of a balloon. Agatha wondered madly whether, if she tied string around his ankles and held him out of the window, he would float up to the sky.

But then brother Guy walked in and Agatha promptly forgot about Peter. Guy Freemont was beautiful. He was tall and slim, with jet-black hair and very blue eyes, a tanned skin and an athlete's body. Agatha judged him to be in his middle thirties. He gave Agatha such a blinding smile that she searched in her brief-case for her notebook to cover her confusion.

They both sat down at the table. 'Now, to business. You come highly recommended,' said Peter.

'I would like to know first,' said Agatha, 'if this meeting to be held by Mary Owen in the village hall is going to pose problems. What if the villagers all decide they don't want the water company?'

'There's nothing they can do,' said Peter, clasping his plump hands covered in black hairs on the table in front of him. 'The spring rises in Mrs Toynbee's garden. Mrs Toynbee is a direct descendant of Miss Jakes, who first channelled the spring out to the road, and Mrs Toynbee has given us her permission.'

Guy opened a folder and slid a piece of artwork in front of Agatha. 'This is what the bottle will look like.' Agatha was surprised to see that the label showed a photograph of the skull with the water gushing out of it. 'Isn't that a bit grim,' she asked, 'particularly in view of the murder?'

'They're not sure it is murder yet,' said Guy. 'Anyway, death's heads and skulls always promote a product. There was a cigarette company that always had something like the shape of a skull in their ads and a brand of gin used to have an ad with the ice cubes in a glass in the shape of a skull.'

'It could be argued,' said Agatha, lighting a cigarette, 'that people who drink and smoke have a death wish. But people who go around drinking gnat's piss like mineral water are usually the healthy type.'

'Not any more,' said Peter. 'They can be reformed alcoholics who still have the death wish. They can be business people at the new fashionable "dry" lunches, or they can be people who just can't stand the taste of the drinking water from the tap, which often smells like swimming pools. But everyone is fascinated by death. Now there needs to be some big event to launch the water. What about taking over some stately home like Blenheim Palace . . .?'

'They'd hardly agree to that, seeing as how they are producing their own water,' Agatha pointed out.

'Perhaps hire a boat and go down the Thames, lots of celebs, lots of booze for the press?' suggested Guy.

'Old hat,' said Agatha. 'I have it, and it'd be a way to get the goodwill of the village. A village fête.'

'Oh, come on,' protested Peter. 'Tacky cakes and home-made jam and women in 1970s Laura Ashley dresses.'

'No, no, listen to me,' said Agatha eagerly. 'Why do you think tourists come to the Cotswolds?'

'Beauty spot?' suggested Peter.

'No, apart from that. The British are as bad as the Americans. The Americans want to believe in the good old days of June Allyson standing at the white picket fence with an apple pie. The British want the rural dream of croquet and skittles and my lord dishing out the prizes. Now usually these village affairs are tacky, I grant you that. But this one could be groomed to look like something out of a Merchant-Ivory film. And I'll get that American film star, Jane Harris, to open it.'

'The Commie?'

'Doesn't matter. Her health and beauty videos sell by the ton. And I'll get some local doddering aristo as well.'

'It could work,' said Guy slowly. 'But we can't control the weather. Crowds aren't going to come to an idyllic English fête if it's pissing down with rain.'

'July's usually a lousy month,' said Agatha.

'Make it for the end of August, before the kids go back to school.'

They discussed the pros and cons of the village fête. Agatha clinched it by pointing out the obvious. It was being marketed as Ancombe water, so where better to have the launch than in Ancombe itself?

'There's one last thing,' said Agatha. 'This meeting in the village hall makes me uneasy. I think we should be there to represent the company. It will be very bad publicity if we end up with the villagers against us. I'll let you know when the meeting is to be held.'

'Guy will go along with you,' said Peter.

Portia entered. 'What is it?' asked Peter.

'That dead man,' said Portia. 'He was murdered.'

'Thank you for telling us.'

Both men waited until the secretary had left. 'Not bad, not bad,' said Peter.

'I can't see how a murder is going to help us.' Agatha looked at them. Then she said slowly, 'Of course, it means there will be a lot of the press at that meeting at the village hall.'

'Exactly,' said Peter. 'And good PR woman that you are, you'd better find a way to swing everyone one hundred per cent behind us. God knows, you're being paid enough.'

Agatha did not like the flick of the whip. 'You get what you pay for when you hire me,' she said evenly. 'Now, if that is all, gentle-men . . .?'

'Bit tasteless that last remark of yours, bro,' murmured Guy after Agatha had left.

'Rolls off that sort of woman. Hard as nails.'

'Sexy with it, though,' said Guy reflectively, staring at the door through which Agatha had just exited.

Agatha arrived back in Carsely to find the press waiting on her doorstep. Mindful of her new role, she invited them all in for drinks and, after describing how she had found the body, put in a good plug for the new water company.

After the press had left, Roy Silver phoned her, eagerly asking how she had got on. 'Very well,' said Agatha, 'although there was a nasty crack from Peter about what they were paying me. I assume you are giving me my usual fee?'

'Told you so. Told them if they wanted qual-ity PR, they had to pay for it.' Agatha told him about the meeting in the village hall.

'I'd better be there, too,' said Roy. A picture of the glamorous Guy rose in Agatha's mind.

'Don't want you around,' she said gruffly.

'Who got you this job?'

'Want it back?'

'Just my little joke, Aggie.'

Agatha hung up.

She realized that if she kept a bright picture of Guy Freemont at the front of her mind, then the image of James Lacey's face was blocked out.

With more cheerfulness and energy than she had felt for a long time, she got out her laptop and began to work busily, writing down the names of journalists she could lure to the opening.

After several hours she stretched and yawned, feeling all the satisfaction of having done a good job. She corrected what she had written, ran it off on the printer and then drove over to Mircester, where she left her papers at the reception desk addressed to the Freemont brothers.

She was driving back through Mircester when she saw Bill Wong just leaving police headquarters. She called to him and stopped the car. He came over.

'What's all the news?' she asked.

'Park and come for a drink. I'll tell you the little I know.'

Agatha parked and walked with him to the George, a gloomy pub in the shade of the abbey.

'It was murder,' said Bill, when they were both settled. 'Someone clubbed him on the back of the head.'

'And laid him backwards in the spring?'

'Yes, but forensic say there is every evidence that he was killed elsewhere, carried to the spring and dumped there.'

'Must have been someone very strong, or more than one.'

'Exactly.'

'And do you think it had something to do with this water business?'

'It certainly looks that way. Mr Struthers was a widower. He lived alone. He has a son down in Brighton who was certainly in Brighton on the night of the murder. He hadn't all that much money to leave. Anyway, the son has a first-class job in computers and has no need of money.'

'What are the other members of the parish council like? Miss Mary Owen, for example.'

'She's quite a commanding personality, tall, thin and leathery. One of those ladies who does good works, not out of any feeling of charity for the less fortunate, but because that's the sort of work ladies do. She's independently wealthy. Some family trust.'

'She's going to make some sort of protest speech. Has she enough personality to sway the villagers?'

'Yes, I should think so.'

'Rats. What about the others?'

'The others against the water company. I'll start with them. Mr Bill Allen. He runs the Ancombe Garden Centre. Very class-conscious and got a bit of an inferiority complex. Father was a farm labourer. So Mr Allen supports all the things he considers Right. Bring back hanging, slaughter the foxes, bring back National Service, that sort of thing.'

'Then I would have thought he would have been all for this water company. Capitalism rules, okay.'

'I believe Miss Owen implied that the Freemont brothers were not gentlemen. Enough said. Now the last of those against is Mr Andy Stiggs, a retired shopkeeper. He's seventy-one and hale and hearty.'

'Maybe there's something in this water after all.'

'Maybe. Anyway, he loves the village and thinks that lorries rumbling through it to take away the water will be a desecration of rural life. Do you remember that supermarket that was proposed for outside Broadway? Well, he got up a petition against it.'

'So what about the ones in favour?'

'There's Mrs Jane Cutler. She's a wealthy widow, sixty-five but doesn't look it. Rumoured to be on her third face-lift. Blonde and shapely. Not very popular in the village but I can't see why. I found her charming. She says the village could do with more tourist trade and Ancombe Water will publicize the village and bring trade in. Then there's Angela Buckley, big strapping girl, forty-eight, but still called a girl. Not married. Rather loud and red-faced, good-natured, but apt to bully the villagers in a patronizing I-know-what's-best-for-the-peasants manner which irritates the hell out of them. Fred Shaw is the last. Electrician. Bossy, sixty, aggressive manner, powerful for his age.'

'Oh, dear,' said Agatha. 'Those against sound more palatable than those for.'

'So what did you make of the Freemonts?'

'Peter Freemont seemed like the usual City businessman. Guy Freemont is charming. Where did they come from?'

'I gather that they ran some export-import company in Hong Kong and got out like everyone else before the Chinese took over. What do you think, Agatha? That they murdered someone to get the publicity?'

'Hardly. I'm sure it's a village matter and it may have nothing to do with the water. People always think of villages as innocent places, not like the towns, but you know what it's like, Bill. An awful lot of nasty passions and jealousies can lie just beneath the surface. I've a feeling in my bones that it's got nothing to do with that spring at all.'

James Lacey was driving past when he saw Agatha and Bill emerge from the George. He longed to be able to call to them, to discuss the murder, but he had to admit to himself that after the way he had been treating Agatha, he could hardly expect a warm reception.

Give Agatha an inch, he thought sourly, and she'll take over your whole life. He drove on, but feeling lonely and excluded and knowing he had only himself to blame.

Two weeks later, with the police no farther on in their murder investigations, Mary Owen's protest meeting was scheduled to take place in the village hall. Agatha arranged that she and Guy Freemont should have places on the platform to present the firm's viewpoint.

Agatha had visited the company's offices in Mircester, presenting outlines for publicizing the water, but each time it was Peter Freemont who saw her. Agatha began to wonder if she would ever see Guy again, but on her last visit Peter had assured her that Guy would call for her before the village meeting so that they could arrive there together.

'Calm down,' Agatha told herself fiercely. 'He's at least twenty years younger than you.' She was torn between trying to look sexy and trying to look businesslike. Common sense at last prevailed on the evening of the meeting, and businesslike won. She put on a smart tailored suit but with high-heeled black patent-leather shoes and a striped blouse, her hair brushed to a high shine, and painted her generous mouth with a Dior lipstick guaranteed not to come off when kissed.

She was ready a good half-hour before Guy was due to arrive. Perfume! She had forgotten to put on any. She rushed upstairs and surveyed the array of bottles on her dressing-table. Rive Gauche. Everyone wore that, particularly now that cut-price shop had opened in Evesham. Champagne? A bit frivolous. Chanel No. 5. Yes, that would do. Safe.

She returned downstairs and checked her sitting-room. Log fire burning brightly, magazines arranged on the coffee-table, drinks on the trolley over at the wall. Ice? Damn, she'd forgotten ice. He wouldn't have time for a drink before they left but perhaps, just perhaps, he might come back with her for one. She went to the kitchen, filled the ice-trays and put them in the freezer.

Then she felt a spot sprouting on her forehead. She tried to tell herself it was all her imagination and rushed upstairs. Her forehead looked unblemished, but she put a little witch hazel on it, just in case. The witch hazel left a round white mark in her mask of foundation cream and powder. She swore and repaired the damage.

By the time the doorbell went, she was feeling hot and frazzled. Guy Freemont stood on the doorstep, black hair gleaming, impeccably tailored, dazzling smile. Agatha felt miserable, like a teenager on her first date.

The village hall was crowded. The press were there in force, not only the locals, but Midlands TV, and some of the nationals. The murder had put Ancombe on the map.

Miss Mary Owen got to her feet to address the crowd. She had a high, autocratic voice and a commanding manner. She was dressed in an old print frock with a droopy hem but wore a fine rope of pearls around her neck.

She began. 'I have been against selling the water all along. It is a disgrace. It is desecration of one of the famous features of the Cotswolds, something that by right belongs to the villagers of Ancombe. You have heard complaints, have you not, about how the life is being drained out of our villages by incomers?' Agatha shifted uneasily. 'I do not think the water should be sold off without the villagers' permission. I suggest we put it here and now to a vote.'

Oh, no, thought Agatha, not before they've heard me. She was about to get to her feet when a woman stood up in the audience. 'It's *my* water,' she said.

'Come up and let's hear you,' called Agatha, glad of the distraction.

The woman was helped up on to the platform. Miss Owen gave her a filthy look but surrendered the microphone to her. 'Who are you?' asked Agatha, lowering the microphone to suit the height of the newcomer.

'I am Mrs Toynbee and the spring is in *my* garden.'

Mrs Toynbee was a small, 'soft' woman, rather like marshmallow, though not plump. She had silver hair which formed a curly aureole about her head. She had the kind of face which romantic novelists call heart-shaped. She had large light blue eyes and fair lashes. Her soft bosom was covered by a glittery evening sweater, white with silver sequins, worn over a long floral skirt. Agatha judged her to be in her forties but when she started to speak, she had a clear, lisping, girlish voice.

'As you all know,' she began, 'I am Mrs Robina Toynbee and I have had a hard time of it since my Arthur passed away.' She paused and carefully dabbed each eye with a small lace-edged handkerchief. Agatha, strictly a man-sized Kleenex woman, marvelled that there were obviously still lace-edged handkerchiefs on the market. 'The water rights are mine to sell,' went on Robina Toynbee.

'But the actual fountain is *outside* your garden!' cried Mary Owen, leaping to her feet.

Robina Toynbee cast her a look of pain and shook her head gently. 'If that is what troubles you, then I have the right to block the spring and they can take the water from my garden.'

'Too difficult,' murmured Guy in Agatha's ear, 'we need that skull for the labels.'

Agatha marched forward. 'If I might have a word, dear.' She edged Robina Toynbee away from the microphone.

'Perhaps I can explain things,' said Agatha. Her eyes flew to where James was standing at the back of the hall, his arms folded. She gave her head a little shake, as if to free it from thoughts of James Lacey. She mentally marshalled her facts and figures and proceeded to bulldoze her audience.

'The company are paying Mrs Toynbee for the water, yes, but they are also paying a generous yearly sum to the parish council which, I gather, if accepted, will go towards the building of a new community hall. Yes, the publicity will bring tourists to the village but tourists will bring trade to the village shops. From nine in the morning each day until the following dawn, the spring will belong to the villagers as it always has.'

Bill Wong leaned back in his seat and smiled appreciatively. It was nice to see Agatha Raisin back on form. He had been worried about her since her break-up with James.

'Wait a bit,' shouted Andy Stiggs. 'I know you, Mrs Raisin. You're one of those incomers, one of those people who are ruining the village character.'

'If it weren't for incomers, you wouldn't have any village character,' said Agatha. 'Those cottages down the lower end of the village, what about them? They were derelict and abandoned for years. Then some enterprising builder did them up, lovingly restored them. Who bought them? Incomers. Who made the gardens pretty again? Incomers.'

'That's because the local people couldn't afford the prices,' panted Andy.

'You mean they're all broke like you, Miss Owen and Mr Bill Allen?'

Agatha winked at the audience and there was an appreciative roar of laughter.

'I must and will have my say.' Bill Allen, the owner of the garden centre, got up and stood in front of the microphone. He was dressed in a hacking jacket, knee-breeches, lovat socks and brogues. A pseud, if ever there was one, thought Agatha, listening to the genteel strangulation of his vowels.

He began to read from a sheaf of papers. It soon became apparent to all in the hall that he had written a speech. A cloud of boredom settled down. Agatha despaired. She wanted the meeting to end on a high note. But how to stop him?

She scribbled something on a piece of paper and handed it to Bill Allen. He glanced at it, turned brick-red and abruptly left the platform.

Gleefully Agatha took his place. 'The other thing I meant to tell you is that to launch the new bottled water, we are going to have a splendid fête right here in Ancombe, a good old-fashioned village fête. Yes, we'll have film stars and people like that present, but I want you to have all your usual stalls, home-made jam, cakes, things like that, and games for the children. It will be the village fête to end all village fêtes. Television will be there, of course, and we will show the world what Ancombe is made of. Won't we?'

She beamed around the audience and was greeted with a roar of applause.

When the vote was taken, the villagers were overwhelmingly in favour of the water company. Many of the villagers belonged to the group of incomers that Andy Stiggs had so despised.

Agatha found her hand being shaken warmly by the councillors who were in favour of the water company – Mrs Jane Cutler, Mr Fred Shaw and Miss Angela Buckley. Angela Buckley, a strapping woman, gave Agatha such a congratulatory thump between the shoulder-blades that she nearly sent her flying off the platform.

'Mission accomplished,' whispered Guy in Agatha's ear. 'Let's get out of here.'

Outside the hall, Guy put his arms around Agatha. 'You were marvellous,' he said. He gave her a kiss full on the mouth. Agatha drew back and stared at him. He was so incredibly handsome and she had felt a definite buzz when he kissed her. She gave a sad little sigh. She had never liked the idea of a toy boy. Better to grow old gracefully.

'What did you write on that note to get the old bore off the platform?' asked Guy.

'I told him his fly was open.'

'Attagirl. Let's have a drink.'

Agatha was suddenly reluctant to take him home. 'Let's go to my local,' she said.

The Red Lion was crowded. The first person Agatha saw was James Lacey, standing at the bar. Agatha looked at his tall, rangy figure, his black hair going grey and handsome face, and felt a lurch in the pit of her stomach. A couple were just vacating a table over at the window, well away from the bar. 'Let's sit over there,' said Agatha quickly.

'I'll get you something,' said Guy. 'What'll it be? I know. Let's see if they have any champagne.'

Agatha was about to protest, to say that she would be happy with a gin and tonic but she saw James staring across at her and smiled up at Guy and said, 'How lovely!'

Guy returned to the table and within a short time the landlord, John Fletcher, came over, carrying the bottle in an ice bucket. The pop of the cork was a festive sound. Several locals stopped by the table to congratulate Agatha on her speech at the village hall. James was left with the company of Mrs Darry.

Agatha could not possibly be interested in that young man, he thought sourly. She was making a fool of herself, sitting there drinking champagne and flirting. She should remember her age! He desperately wanted to talk to her about the murder but did not know how to break the ice that he himself had caused to form.

He talked as civilly as he could to Mrs Darry and then abruptly left the pub.

An hour later, he heard a car drive up and stop outside Agatha's cottage. He rushed to the little upstairs window on the landing which overlooked Agatha's cottage. Agatha opened the car door. Guy Freemont was at the wheel. He could see that clearly because the light sprang on inside the car when Agatha opened the door. Guy put his hand on Agatha's arm and said something. He saw Agatha smile and say something in reply. Then she went into her cottage and Guy drove off. At least he hadn't gone in with her.

He waited the next day expecting Agatha to call him, to suggest they investigate the murder together, but nobody called at all. He went out and bought all the newspapers. The locals had given the meeting a good show and there was even a photo of Agatha on the front page of the *Cotswold Journal*, but the nationals only carried small paragraphs.

James began to feel restless and bored. He decided to investigate the murder himself.

After several tries, he managed to get Bill Wong on the phone, and finding he was off duty that evening, offered to buy him dinner. Bill agreed. His beloved Sharon had said she had to wash her hair.

James had chosen a Chinese restaurant, recently opened. The restaurant was quiet and the food good.

'I'm fascinated by this murder,' said James. 'Any idea who did it?'

'We're ferreting into backgrounds at the moment, and checking up on movements. You would think that somebody might have seen that body dumped at the spring, heard a car or something, but so far we've drawn a blank. It's funny, you sitting there being interested in a case. It would be quite like old times, except that you haven't got Agatha with you.'

'I assume she's too busy with her new job,' said James flatly.

'Is that what she said?'

'I don't know. I haven't spoken to her.'

'Why?'

'I really don't want to discuss Agatha. Do you think one of the members of the parish council might have done it?'

'They're all too respectable,' mourned Bill. 'Still, you never know. It's amazing what you find out about people once you start digging into their past. I can't really tell you what we've got so far because it's all confidential. If you want to know anything, you'll need to ferret around yourself, provided you don't get under the feet of the police.'

'I don't trust that water company,' said James. 'I don't like that younger one, Guy Freemont.'

Bill's eyes crinkled up in a smile. 'No, you wouldn't, would you?'

'Don't be ridiculous. I'm not jealous.'

'If you say so.'

'So who are they? Where did these Freemont brothers come from?'

'They had an import-export business in Hong Kong.'

'Oh, yeah? Drugs?'

'No, clothes. Cheap clothes going out and more expensive clothes for the rich coming in.'

'I bet they ran sweatshops.'

'Sure you're not jealous? So far we can find out nothing against them. They made their pile in Hong Kong, all legit, and came back to Britain recently, just before the Chinese take-over. But we're still investigating.'

'Why water? Why Ancombe?'

'Mr Peter Freemont said he happened to notice the spring during a weekend in the Cotswolds and thought a mineral-water company might be a good idea.'

'So they bump someone off who might have stopped their plans?'

'It's hardly a good advertisement.'

'It got the name Ancombe Water in all the papers.'

'So it did. But, like I said, hardly a good advertisement. Anyone buying the water will remember the body was found lying with the head in the basin, and our Agatha's vivid description in the newspapers of the blood swirling around in the moonlight. I think you can forget them. Why don't you ask Agatha? She must have got to know them pretty well.'

'I told you. For once in her life, Agatha seems too busy to concentrate on murder.'

While Bill and James were dining, Agatha was having a pleasant dinner with Guy Freemont. He encouraged her to talk about herself, flattered her ability in public relations and then asked her what a 'city girl' like herself was doing buried in the Cotswolds.

'I sometimes wonder,' said Agatha ruefully. 'But you get used to the safe life, the sleepy life, and it's so beautiful, particularly at this time of year. It's beautiful everywhere you look. Have you seen that purple wisteria in Broadway? The blooms are so magnificent. It's a wonder it doesn't cause accidents, with so many drivers putting on their brakes to have a better look.'

'But don't you miss the excitement of London?'

'London has changed so rapidly. Last time I was up, I had a meal in a restaurant in Goodge Street and decided afterwards to walk down Tottenham Court Road to get the tube for the Central Line. There were beggars and drug addicts all the way along and shapeless bundles of clothes huddled in doorways. When I got off the tube at Notting Hill to change on to the Circle Line for Paddington, a man, drunk as a skunk, tried to throw himself under the next train. This big burly man snatched him back in the nick of time and marched him up the escalators to the ticket collector. At the top, the would-be suicide wrenched free, vaulted the turnstile and vanished into the night. His rescuer said to the ticket collector, "That man just tried to throw himself in front of the train!" The ticket collector shrugged and looked bored. Didn't do anything about it. I was glad to get back down here. I don't belong in London any more. It can be a lonely place.'

He took her hand and gave it a warm squeeze. 'Any romance in your life?'

'Nothing that I want to talk about,' said Agatha as his thumb began to stroke the palm of her hand. Her mind raced. I can't be doing this, she thought frantically. I'm too old. I don't have stretch marks, but I have love handles and my boobs don't perk up the way they used to.

When he drove her home, he stopped outside her cottage and, leaning across, planted a warm kiss on her mouth. Agatha blinked at him, dazed and shaken. 'I'm going up to London for a few days,' he said softly. 'I'll call you when I get back. You've been working like a beaver. Why don't you take a few days off and relax?'

'I'll do that,' said Agatha huskily.

She let herself into the cottage and stood in her hallway, her knees shaking.

You are ridiculous, she told herself fiercely. She peered in the hall mirror at the lines around her mouth, at the lines on her neck.

The phone rang, making her jump. It was Bill Wong. 'Been out?' he asked.

'Yes, Bill. I had dinner with Guy Freemont. Got anyone for the murder yet?'

'Not yet. I had dinner with James Lacey.'

Agatha went very still. 'And?'

'And he seems hell-bent on playing the amateur sleuth again.'

'He won't get very far without me.'

'He supposes you're too busy to be interested.'

'Too right. In the murder and in him.'

'If, on the other hand, you do hear any gossip, let me know, Agatha. We seem to be at a dead end.'

Agatha then asked about his girlfriend and his parents, and after a few more moments' conversation, rang off.

She had a few days off. She could not bear the idea of James's finding out anything and taking all the glory. It would do no harm to drop in on some of the parish councillors in the morning, just to see if she could find out anything.

Chapter Three

Agatha decided to start off with one of the councillors friendly to the water company. That way, it might be easier to get gossip. She looked up Mrs Jane Cutler in the phone book and noted down her address. She hesitated, wondering whether to phone first, but then decided it would be a better ploy just to land on the doorstep.

Mrs Cutler lived in Wisteria Cottage in Ancombe, near the church. Wisteria Cottage turned out not to have any wisteria in evidence, nor was it a cottage. It was a modern bungalow with double glazing and ruched curtains. The lawn was a severe square of green grass surrounded by regimented flowers which looked as if they had been measured to stand exactly four inches apart from each other, no more, no less.

Agatha knew that Mrs Cutler was aged sixty-five and did not look it, but she was startled again at the appearance of the woman who opened the door to her and confirmed that she was, indeed, Mrs Cutler.

Mrs Jane Cutler had expensively blonded hair, her skin was smooth and her figure excellent. Only the eyes were old and watchful and the wrists and ankles had that fragile, brittle appearance of old age. No plastic surgeon had yet found the way to make eyes look youthful. She must be very rich indeed, thought Agatha, as she followed her indoors. It took a mint to look like that.

She was wearing a clinging wool jersey dress of goldy-brown with a colourful Hermès scarf at her neck.

'I am so glad to see you, Mrs Raisin,' she said. 'Such a silly fuss about some water! I'll just go and get us some coffee. Shan't be a tick.'

Agatha looked round the sitting-room, which was furnished in Bastard Country House. Hunting prints on the wall, chintz on the sofa, expensive fake fire where gas flames flickered among fake logs, *Country Life* and *The Lady* on the coffee-table, very new oriental rugs spread over the hair-cord fitted carpet.

In a short time Jane Cutler reappeared with coffee and biscuits on a tray. Agatha reflected bitchily that with the money that had gone into maintaining her appearance, Jane Cutler could have bought a real country mansion.

After the coffee had been served, Agatha said, 'I do not understand why any of the councillors should be against the water company. Such a fuss about nothing.'

'Oh, you know what village people can be like,' said Mrs Cutler. 'So narrow-minded. Now I have always had broad vision. And my vision tells me that this water-company business is a good idea. I can understand why you work for them. I suppose people like you have to go on earning money, no matter what their age.'

'I –' began Agatha furiously.

'Have a biscuit. You obviously are a sensible woman and can't be bothered with all this silly dieting.'

Now I know why people don't like you, thought Agatha, feeling her skirt-band tightening against her waist and wondering again if people could suffer from instant psychosomatic fat.

'I can't help thinking,' ventured Agatha, deciding not to rise to insults, 'that this awful murder might have something to do with the row about the water. I mean, why would anyone want to bump off a nice man like Mr Struthers?'

A merry laugh. 'Dear Mrs Raisin, who gave you the odd idea that Mr Struthers was a nice man?'

'I mean,' floundered Agatha, 'there was surely nothing about him that bad to make anyone want to murder him.'

'We-ell, I probably shouldn't be saying this . . .'

Agatha waited patiently, convinced that nothing in this world could make Mrs Cutler refrain from saying anything nasty about anyone else.

'You see, Mr Struthers owned the paddock which borders on Angela Buckley's father's land. Do you know our Angela? Great strapping monster. Big powerful hands. Well, the Buckleys wanted to buy that paddock. Take it from me, dear, land greed is a worse addiction than drink or drugs or' – her glance flicked up and down Agatha's figure – 'chocolate. There was quite a stormy scene at the last council meeting and it wasn't about the water. Angela said that Mr Struthers never used that paddock, that it was a waste of land and that the only reason he wasn't selling it was out of spite. Mr Struthers said it was no wonder she had never married, she was such a frump, and it was no wonder Percy Cutler had jilted her almost at the altar, and Angela slapped his face! My dear, we had to *pull her off!*'

'Cutler,' said Agatha slowly. 'Percy Cutler? Your son?'

'No, my late husband.'

'But –'

'Oh, there was an age difference, I admit, but what does that matter when there is real love? When poor Percy died of cancer, that bitch Angela said I had known that he had cancer and had only married him to get my hands on his money.'

'How dreadful,' said Agatha faintly.

'I pointed out to her that the husband before Percy, my Charles, had been very rich and I had no need to marry again for money'

'How many husbands have you had?' blurted out Agatha.

'Just the three.'

'And what did the first two die of?'

'Cancer. So sad. I nursed them all devotedly.'

It might be considered a brand-new way of gold digging, thought Agatha. Marry a man who knows he's got cancer and not long to live.

'So you think,' she said aloud, 'that perhaps Angela or her father might have murdered Mr Struthers. But why? How would that give them the land?'

'Because the son and the father never got on. The son, Jeffrey, was always nagging his father to sell them the land. They'll get it now.'

There was a silence while Agatha digested this news. 'Anyone else have it in for old Struthers?'

'Well, everyone knows about Andy Stiggs.'

'Not me,' said Agatha fervently.

'Of course, you're one of those incomers from . . . where? Birmingham, maybe?'

Agatha coloured angrily. She had been brought up in a Birmingham slum and had done her best with clothes and accent to bury her past forever.

'London,' she snapped.

'Really? I could have sworn there was a trace of Brummie there. Anyway, the late Mrs Struthers, away back before God was born, was the belle of Ancombe. I never saw it. One of those rather common blowsy creatures with a loud laugh, you know – the kind you see on a bar-stool in a road-house, skirt hitched up, laughing insanely when not taking sips out of one of those drinks that come with an umbrella sticking out of the glass. Andy Stiggs was passionately in love with her and swore Robert Struthers had lured her away.'

'So does anyone know which way Mr Struthers meant to vote?'

'Oh, who cares? We all got tired of him nodding his stupid head and saying, "I'll make up my mind when the time comes." Now if you'll excuse me, I have to change. I am expecting a gentleman caller.'

Feeling quite stunned by all this gossip, Agatha made her way out. She got into her car and was about to drive off when she was suddenly overcome with curiosity to see who this gentleman caller might be. She drove as far as the end of the road and parked under a lilac tree where she could still command a good view of Jane Cutler's front door.

She waited and waited and after three quarters of an hour was just beginning to decide that Jane had used a fiction of a gentleman caller to get rid of her when she saw a familiar car drawing up outside her house and a familiar figure got out. James Lacey!

Agatha's hand tightened angrily on the steering wheel. So he, too, had begun investigations!

She drove along the village street, stopped at the newspaper shop and asked for directions to the Buckley farm, and headed off.

Agatha was wary of farms, considering them full of livestock of which she knew nothing and snapping dogs. The farmhouse was more of a country mansion, being a Georgian building four storeys high, well maintained.

The door was standing open. There came the sound of voices from within.

'Hello!' shouted Agatha.

The voices stopped, then there was the sound of a chair being scraped back, then booted feet.

Angela Buckley appeared. 'It's our heroine,' she cried. 'Come along in.'

Agatha followed her into a stone-flagged kitchen. Three men sat at the table with cups of tea. 'That's my father,' said Angela, jerking her head at a grey-haired man, 'and that's Joe and Ben, they work for us. Sit down and have a coffee. This lot were just going back to work.'

The farmer picked up a cap from the back of his chair and put it on. 'Saw you the other night, Mrs Raisin,' he said. 'You told 'em.'

He went out, followed by the two men. Angela and Agatha sat down at the table.

'I've just been to see Jane Cutler,' said Agatha.

'Oh, the slurry with the fringe on top. Why did you go to see her?'

Agatha decided to plunge right in. 'I wanted to see if I could find out anything about the murder.'

'What's that got to do with you? That's police business.'

'But as I am working for the water company, it is in their interest to get this murder cleared up as quickly as possible.'

'So what did the raddled old bitch have to say for herself?'

'She more or less said you did it.'

'There's no end to that woman's venom. She's had so many face-lifts and been so stretched that every time she opens her mouth her arsehole gapes. What reason should I have for murdering old Struthers?'

'The paddock.'

'Oh, that. It had become a bit of a joke between us. He would say, "You'll need to

62

wait until I'm dead." Oh, lor'. Doesn't that sound awful?'

'But there was no real feeling about it?'

'There was from time to time. He didn't need that paddock, and he was a stubborn old codger. But actually he'd call round here quite a lot. We were friends.'

'So who could have done it? Was it to stop him voting for or against? Did any of you know which way he meant to vote?'

'No, he enjoyed teasing us.'

'What about Mary Owen? Tell me about her.'

'She always wanted to head the parish council but we wouldn't let her. She's so bossy. I think in her way she kept us all together, despite our differences. We all hated her.'

Agatha wondered whether to broach the subject of the late Percy Cutler, but decided against it. Her own heartache over James had made her unusually sensitive to another woman's feelings.

'We've always had fights over something or another,' Angela was saying, 'but they all die away after a while.' She looked at Agatha and her round weather-beaten face suddenly turned hard. 'Drop this amateur murder investigation. All you'll do is stir up a lot of muck . . . and you might get hurt.'

'Is that a warning?' asked Agatha, gathering up her handbag.

'Yes, it is. A friendly warning.'

Agatha said goodbye and went out to where her car was parked in the farmyard. As she drove off, she looked in the rear-view mirror. Angela was standing, her hands on her hips, watching her go. Her face was grim.

Agatha went home and phoned Bill Wong and told him of both conversations, the one with Jane Cutler and the one with Angela. Bill groaned. 'This opens up a messy field of research. Let me know if you find out anything else.'

'What, no warning to keep out of it?'

'I need all the help I can get on this one.'

James Lacey phoned Bill Wong later. 'I went to see that Cutler woman as a start,' he said. 'I'm afraid there's nothing there. According to her the members of the parish council all love one another. I must admit I found her very charming.'

'That's not what our Agatha found out,' said Bill gleefully.

There was a short silence and then James said, 'What do you mean?'

Bill repeated what Agatha had told him.

'Mrs Cutler said nothing of that to me,' complained James.

'Probably she reserves all her nice manners for us gentlemen. I found her charming as well. You should join forces with Agatha.'

'I'll think about it,' said James curtly.

But he took several days to think about it and by that time Guy Freemont had phoned up Agatha and invited her out for dinner.

'I'm afraid I'm busy tonight, James,' said Agatha, noticing with irritation that her hand holding the telephone receiver was trembling. 'Got a dinner date.'

'Oh, well, what about if I pop round this afternoon?'

'Got an engagement for this afternoon,' said Agatha. 'Look, I'll call you. Bye.'

She sat down on the stairs. Why, oh, why had James decided to contact her just when she was booked to have dinner with Guy and had made an appointment with a beautician in Evesham for that afternoon?

James was the same age as she, and if she had been going out with him, then she would not be rushing off to the beautician to have electrodes put on her face and neck to try to reduce the wrinkles.

This was what came of dating a much younger man and a handsome man at that. Somehow, with the work for the water company, and then the prospect of going out with

Guy, she had not thought much about the murder, nor had she investigated it further.

But the gloss of that date with Guy had been definitely tarnished and it was a gloomy Agatha who drove into Evesham. She had picked out a beautician from the Yellow Pages.

Evesham was an odd town, reflected Agatha, as she made her way up a narrow staircase to the beautician's. All over the town, shops had closed down and the boarded-up fronts had been decorated with paintings of old Evesham shops by a local artist. If this goes on, thought Agatha, Evesham will soon be a town of paintings. No shops. And yet, here was this beautician who appeared to have the latest in beauty treatments, and along the road, a drugstore was doing a brisk trade in cut-price French perfume. It should have been a bustling, prosperous town. So much traffic, so many houses being built. But quite a lot of people were on the dole and didn't seem much interested in getting off it. A local fruit-packing company was bussing in workers from Wales because the locals wouldn't take up the jobs.

Agatha opened the door of the beautician's and went in.

The beautician, called Rosemary, was refreshingly maternal and non-threatening. Agatha, who had been expecting some anorectic creature who would make her feel frumpy, began to relax.

That was until the electrodes were attached to her face and neck and switched on. 'It's a good thing I know this is a beauty treatment,' muttered Agatha. 'If I was in a police station in a totalitarian state, I would think it was torture and tell them everything.' But she booked up a further nine appointments.

For good measure, she had her eyebrows shaped and her eyelashes dyed. She walked down the stairs and along the High Street, squinting sideways at her reflection in shop windows to see if she looked any younger.

It seemed to take ages to get home, because she had forgotten about the building of the Broadway bypass and the traffic lights on Fish Hill. The bypass would surely benefit Broadway by taking away all the huge rumbling trucks that daily shook the old buildings of the village, and yet it was very sad to see the trees on Fish Hill cut down for the new road and the scarred earth on either side where sheep so lately had peacefully grazed.

Once home, she began the long preparation necessary to any middle-aged woman who is dating a younger man, although she kept reminding herself fiercely that it was only a business partnership.

By the time, she had applied the last of her make-up and stood before the mirror wondering if the low-cut fine wool red dress was too gaudy, she felt a wrench of real pain. Instead of going through all this, she could have been talking to James about the case, building bridges, getting back to the old warmth and closeness.

When Guy called to pick her up, she had lost all interest in him.

Guy drove her to Oxford, parked in the underground car park in Gloucester Green and then escorted her to a French restaurant. It turned out to be one of those ones with a delicious menu and lousy food. A good way of dieting, thought Agatha, would be just to enjoy the prose on the menu and then not order anything.

Agatha had ordered breast of duck stuffed with spinach on a bed of warm rocket which translated itself into a piece of rubber stuffed with decaying vegetable matter, and rocket must be surely the most overrated vegetable in the world. It always tasted to Agatha like weeds.

They talked about various journalists and which would be more inclined to give them a good show. Agatha had already arranged various lunches in London with journalists. Guy said the new colour brochures advertising the water would be ready in a couple of days' time and that he would save Agatha a trip to Mircester and run over with them.

They drank a bottle of highly priced indifferent wine, but there was enough alcohol in it to mellow Agatha. After coffees and two brandies, she felt happy to be in the company of this well-tailored and handsome man.

When the bill was presented, Guy began patting his pockets. Then he gave Agatha a rueful boyish smile. 'Damn, I've left my wallet at home.'

'It's all right, I'll pay,' said Agatha, thinking not for the first time that the majority of Englishmen were as tight as the bark on the tree.

He drove her back home. James heard the car arrive and leaped for the side window of his cottage. Guy, his black hair gleaming in the light over Agatha's door, took her keys from her and unlocked the door for her. James held his breath. Then Guy followed Agatha in. James waited and waited. He drew a chair up to the window and waited. Lights from the downstairs window shone out into Agatha's small square of front garden. At last they went off and the hall light went on. Then the hall light was switched off and the light on the stairs switched on. Then the light from behind the drawn curtains of Agatha's bedroom lit up the garden.

'Silly woman,' he muttered, but still he waited. When the light in Agatha's bedroom was switched off and no Guy could be seen leaving the house, James went to bed.

* * *

Agatha came awake suddenly the next morning. She couldn't believe she had actually had sex with Guy. What on earth was up with her? Was she trying to prove that at her age she could still do it without a map?

She lay and listened to the silence of the house. Please let him be gone! That was the hell about being middle-aged. There was all the fear of trying to get to the bathroom to slap on make-up before he caught a glimpse of her unadorned face. But there was no sound but the wind blowing through the heavy purple lilac blossoms outside the window.

She got out of bed, feeling stiff and sore. After a deep bath, she felt better. She made up carefully and dressed, and then ripped the sheets off the bed and carried them down to the washing machine in the kitchen. She fed her cats and let them out into the sunshine of the garden.

There was a knock at the door. Perhaps it was James! But it was only Mrs Bloxby, the vicar's wife.

'I've brought you some home-made marmalade,' she said. 'You are looking very well this morning.'

'Thanks,' said Agatha, leading the way into the kitchen and nervously eyeing the laundry basket of sheets she had left on the kitchen floor. 'I'll just pop these in the machine and then we'll have coffee.'

'So you've been out with that young man from the water company?' said Mrs Bloxby. One is never too old to blush. Agatha bent over the washing machine and loaded it. 'How did you know?' she asked over her shoulder.

'Mrs Darry was round at the vicarage first thing this morning to tell me that he had gone in with you after driving you home and hadn't come out again. You know what villages are like.'

'That cow lives at the other end of the village!'

'But she has a nasty little yapping dog and dogs are very useful for walking about the streets at night by someone who is more interested in other people's lives than they are in their own.'

Agatha plugged in the coffee percolator. 'So I went to bed with him. Does that shock you?'

'No dear, but it probably shocks you. Women of our generation never got used to casual sex. Now young people these days just seem to go and do it without feeling any loss of dignity at all. And yet it is a most undignified performance, unless one is in love, of course.'

'I suppose that Darry woman will spread it all round the village and James will get to hear of it.'

'Is that so very bad? He has been neglecting

you. He cannot expect you to carry a torch for him forever.'

Agatha poured two cups of coffee and sat down wearily at the kitchen table. 'I feel a fool. I think Guy Freemont is a taker. He took me to a quite dreadful French restaurant in Oxford, very expensive, and then said he had forgotten his wallet.'

'Perhaps he did.'

'I doubt it. I have endured a long series of dinners and lunches with men who forget their wallets or go to the men's room the minute the bill comes up.'

'Then I suggest you forget your own cards and money the next time you go out. He might find he has his wallet on him after all.'

Agatha grinned. 'I'll try that. No more trouble about the water, is there?'

'As a matter of fact, there is.'

'What?'

'You've heard of Greenpeace and Friends of the Earth?'

'Yes.'

'There's a new lot nobody heard of before this year. Save Our Foxes.'

'But they're hunt saboteurs!'

'Yes, but they are organizing a march on the spring for this Saturday.'

'What's it got to do with them?'

'They say it is an example of how capitalism is ruining rural life.'

'Bollocks.'

'Quite. They will not get a welcome because the water company has started hiring staff, and young people from Ancombe are getting first priority.'

'I hope this won't mean bad publicity.'

'I think it will mean some violence and I hope the police can control it. You see, most of these protesters come from the towns and they do not seem to understand country life. I am talking about the genuine protesters, usually serious and mild-mannered people. But they often find their protests are hijacked by thugs looking for a punch-up.'

'I'd better be there,' said Agatha.

'Do be careful.'

'I will.'

After the vicar's wife had left, Agatha sat down to bring her expenses for the water company up-to-date, knowing of old the horror of leaving expense accounts to the last minute. Then she opened her handbag and took out the bill from the French restaurant. She neatly typed into her computer, 'To entertaining Mr Guy Freemont, ninety-two pounds, plus ten pounds gratuity,' and grinned as she ran it off on the printer.

* * *

Guy Freemont and his brother were sitting discussing business two days later when their accountant, James Briggs, came in.

'Yes, Briggs, what is it?' asked Peter.

'There is an item on Mrs Raisin's expense account I thought you might like to consider?'

'What's up with the old bat?' demanded Peter. 'Charging us for clothes or make-up, or what?'

'It's this.' James Briggs placed a list of figures in front of the two brothers. 'Everything seems in order except that I find it odd that she has put in an expensive restaurant bill for entertaining Mr Guy Freemont.'

Peter tapped it. 'What's this, Guy?'

'I did invite her out for dinner, but forgot my wallet.'

'Again? Let it go this time, Briggs.'

When the accountant had left, Peter said wrathfully, 'She's a good PR. Don't screw her around until we get this water safely launched.'

'I forgot my wallet,' said Guy. 'That's all.'

Agatha had learned that the protest was to take place at eleven o'clock on Saturday morning. She was there in good time. Other people were gathered around. Mary Owen came straight up to Agatha. 'You're not going to get away with this,' she snarled.

'Oh, sod off,' said Agatha. 'Is this protest your idea?'

'No, but it goes to show that people all over Britain are not going to sit back and see the life of the country ruined.'

Agatha shrugged and moved away, only to bump into Bill Allen. 'You'd better be careful,' he said in his odd, strangled Savoyard voice. 'You have stirred up deep feelings.'

'Are you threatening me?'

'Just a warning, Mrs Raisin.'

A silence fell on the crowd as eleven o'clock came and went. Agatha suddenly saw James's tall figure at the edge of the crowd. She longed to join him but was frightened of being snubbed. And yet he had phoned her. She was just edging her way towards him when someone shouted, 'Here they come!'

A small procession was heading towards the spring. At the front were gentle-faced middle-aged people, but behind them came burly young men with tattoos, camouflage jackets, earrings, and trouble written all over them. Five policemen were standing in front of the spring.

The onlookers cleared a way for them. A woman with a face like that of a worried sheep turned to face the crowd and took out a sheaf of papers.

'We are here,' she said in a wavering voice,

'to protest against the commercialization of this spring. Our village life must be protected.'

'Where do you live?' shouted Agatha.

The woman blinked, opened and shut her mouth, then held on to her notes more firmly and went on. 'As I was saying, we must protect –'

'Where do you live?' demanded Agatha again.

'Shut your face!' shouted one of the tattooed young men.

'No, I will not shut up,' yelled Agatha. 'Does this woman know anything about village life? Or did you all come from Birmingham or London to make trouble?'

The tattooed man began to work his way towards Agatha. He had thick lips and a beetling brow. Agatha wondered whether to flee. But the police were there. And James – James, who had miraculously appeared at her side.

'I think she should answer the question,' came Jane Cutler's voice. 'These protesters look as if they come from the slums of Birmingham. They are strangers to the country, and to the bath, from the smell of them.'

'That's torn it,' muttered James.

The truculent young man had reached Agatha. 'You shut your mouth or I'll shut it for you.'

James moved in front of Agatha. 'You'll get nowhere with your protest uttering threats.'

In time, James saw the bulletlike head moving forward to head-butt him and jumped to one side. Several women screamed. The police moved forward.

A scrawny woman wearing, of all things, a flak jacket, grabbed hold of Jane Cutler and pulled her hair. Jane screamed like a banshee. The police wrestled the woman to the ground. Sirens sounded in the distance as police reinforcements began to arrive.

Agatha's would-be assailant was trying to land a punch on James. James was dodging and weaving, knowing that these days if he landed a punch on the man himself, he could well end up in court for assault.

The spokeswoman for the demonstrators was now crying helplessly. Agatha saw Mrs Bloxby go up to her, say a few words and then begin to lead the weeping woman away.

Police swept into the crowd. They grabbed the young man who had been trying to hit James and carried him off. 'Pigs!' he was screaming. And as he was dragged backwards, his burning eyes looked straight at Agatha and he shouted, 'I'll fix you.'

'Come along,' said James, taking Agatha's arm. 'We need a drink.'

'Where? Here? In the village?'

'No, let's go back to Carsely.'

The Red Lion was quiet and they found a table in a corner next to the log fire which had been lit, for the day was cold.

'Bill Wong told me you had better success with Jane Cutler than I had.'

'So he told you?'

'Why not? I hope we are not going to work against each other.'

'I don't think I'm going to be working on this at all,' said Agatha. 'I've got to go up to London next week. Got a lot of journalists to see.'

'Oh, so I'm on my own?'

'For the moment. It certainly looks that way.' Agatha wondered what on earth had prompted her to say such a thing. Had she kept her mouth shut, they could have gone on discussing the case.

'I'll see what I can do,' said James. He looked at her thoughtfully. 'Just a friendly word of advice, Agatha. Don't take this the wrong way.'

Now, Agatha knew as well as anybody that when someone says, 'Don't take this the wrong way,' the best thing to do is to stop them saying anything, but something inside her seemed to have pressed the 'destruct' button that morning, so she said, 'Go on.'

'I think you are making a spectacle of yourself with that young man from the water company. This new taste in young men is a bit

78

sad. There was Charles in Cyprus and now this one. It doesn't matter if the man is wealthy; toy boy is the label stuck on him if he consorts with a woman as old as you.'

Agatha's face had turned a muddy colour with hurt.

She stood up, knocking her chair backwards as she did so. 'Damn you,' she said in a choked voice.

James got up as well. 'Look here, Agatha. I only –'

'Shut up!' screamed Agatha. 'Just shut up!'

As she raced out of the door, she saw Mrs Darry standing at the bar, her face avid with curiosity.

James slowly finished his drink, aware all the time of curious eyes turned in his direction, of the fact that Mrs Darry was eagerly grabbing hold of every newcomer and whispering fiercely.

He rose and went out and walked slowly home. He could not admit to himself he had been at fault, or that his remarks had been prompted by jealousy. He was overwhelmed instead by a burning desire to find out something about this murder. Then perhaps, just perhaps, he would tell Agatha what he had found out. Her scene in the pub had been unforgivable.

Chapter Four

The following Monday, Agatha packed her bags and headed for London. She had a heavy week's work ahead of her talking to journalists. James's words still burnt and hurt.

The Charles he had referred to was Sir Charles Fraith, a baronet in his forties with whom Agatha had enjoyed a fling in Cyprus. Although she had only gone to bed with Charles out of pique over James's own unfaithfulness, she knew he had no more forgiven her for that brief affair than for trying to marry him when she was already married.

Charles had phoned Agatha several times since their return from abroad, but she had always told him she was too busy to see him and so he had stopped calling.

She was glad she was leaving. There was a police force to cope with murder investigations. She would concentrate on her work and forget James and forget murder and forget Carsely for a little.

She passed a busy week in London, cajoling journalists into promising to come to the fête. Instead of bringing the new brochures over to Carsely as he had promised, Guy had sent them to her hotel in London.

At the end of her week's work, Agatha finally accepted an invitation to lunch from Roy Silver.

Roy took her to an old City restaurant where the public relations company they both worked for had an account. It was quiet and stately, mahogany and brass and solid old-fashioned City food. It was hardly Roy's scene. He would have preferred a trendy wine bar full of bright young things, but he had no intention of paying for the meal when he could charge it to the firm.

Roy was wearing an Armani suit which looked a size too large for his thin figure. His tie was a noisy psychedelic glare in the gloom of the conservative restaurant.

They both ordered roast beef, Agatha eating hers with every appearance of enjoyment and Roy poking at his and occasionally eating little nibbles.

They discussed various aspects of the fête, who was definitely going to attend, who was iffy. Then Roy leaned back in the chair and ran his fingers through his hair. He had a thin face, a weedy body and sharp clever eyes. After working for Agatha and taking up his present job, he had adopted a more sober style of dress – if you discounted the tie – and the hole in his left ear where he used to wear an ear-ring was the only mute sign of his discarded image.

'You haven't mentioned James Lacey or murder all week, Aggie,' he said.

'Been too busy,' said Agatha. 'I wonder if I should have a pudding?'

'It's your waistline, sweetie.'

Agatha signalled the waiter. 'I'll have the spotted dick.'

Roy giggled. 'What a name for a pudding! Sounds like a case of syphilis. So, like I said, how's murder?'

'I told you, I've been too busy.'

'Not like you. What's happened to that famous curiosity of yours?'

'I've decided to do my job and leave the police to do theirs.'

'So what happened with you and James in Cyprus?'

'He went off with a tart. He claims it was all part of his investigations into drugs.'

'And you don't think so? Come on, Aggie. Our James isn't the kind to go with tarts for any reason other than investigation. Too much of a puritan.'

'Well, I had a bit of a fling with someone and he got miffed.'

'Naughty old Aggie. You really ought to do something about this murder.'

'Why?'

'Be a good bit of publicity if you found out who did it. I mean, haven't you got one teensy-weensy suspect?'

'There's one I would like it to be.'

'Give.'

'Some old bat called Jane Cutler. She's a walking monument to the plastic surgeon and the beautician. In her sixties, but all face-lifted. She's poison. The things that go on in villages. She seems to specialize in marrying men on their last legs with cancer and then benefiting in their wills. She's a parish councillor. One of the others, Angela Buckley, fortyish, strapping, was keen on the late Percy Cutler, but the older Jane Cutler snatched him out of her grasp. Actually, Angela warned me off.'

'So you think it might have nothing to do with the water?'

'I don't know.'

'Anyone else warn you off? Any trouble?'

'Andy Stiggs, another councillor, one of the ones who are against the water company. He warned me off when there was that ruckus from Save Our Foxes.'

'Who the hell are they?'

'Some environment group who have transferred their attention from the plight of foxes to the sacrilege of taking water out of the

84

spring. Usual lot. Nice people really interested in a batty way in protecting village life followed by the usual trouble-making skinheads. There was a bit of a dust-up. James nearly got hurt protecting me.'

'So is he doing anything about finding out about anything?'

'I don't think he's interested in anything other than insulting me.'

'Shows he's still interested, Aggie. Wouldn't insult you otherwise. Why don't you ask me down for the weekend? We could ferret around together.'

Agatha opened her mouth to refuse and then closed it again. She did not know if Guy meant to have an affair with her, or whether it was to be regarded as a one-night stand. Suddenly the idea of going back on her own made her feel vulnerable. Roy could be tiresome and malicious, but they had known each other since he had started work for her as an office boy.

'Yes, all right,' she said. 'I suppose it might be interesting to trot around and ask a few questions.'

'You'd better eat that stodgy pudding. It's getting cold.'

Agatha regretted her invitation when she met Roy at Paddington Station on Saturday morning. He was dressed in skin-tight jeans and a black leather jacket and talking into a mobile phone, looking around all the while to see if people noticed he was talking on a mobile phone, just as if millions of people hadn't got the damn things, which Agatha thought had been expressly designed to irritate the travelling public.

'If you use that on the train,' snarled Agatha when he had rung off, 'I'll throw it out of the window. And you're only in your twenties. I thought men only went in for jeans and black leather when they hit the male menopause.'

'And I thought middle-aged women only took to eating roast beef and fattening pudding when they thought they were past attracting *anyone*.'

'Oh, stop bitching,' snapped Agatha.

She passed the journey to Moreton-in-Marsh by ignoring Roy and reading a novel set in the Cotswolds about middle-class, middle-aged infidelity, marvelling as she did so at her own attitude that the well-off middle classes should not have any passions and remembering the days of her youth when it was the lower classes who were supposed to be immune to the sensitivities of soul suffered by their betters. At one point in the journey, Roy's phone rang but he retreated with it down the carriage before Agatha's basilisk glare.

Bright yellow fields of oil seed rape slid past the carriage windows, and lilac trees heavy with blossom leaned down over railway embankments. With that now familiar feeling of coming home, Agatha gathered up her belongings as the train finally slid into Moreton-in-Marsh Station.

With Roy carrying his own weekend bag and Agatha's suitcase, they made their way to Agatha's car. The sky was blue and birds sang in the trees bordering the station car park. Flower baskets moved in the light breeze.

'When I'm as old as you,' said Roy, 'I'll move down here.'

Feeling ancient, Agatha drove off, negotiating the heavy traffic in Moreton and then swinging out along the A44 and up the long steep slope through Bourton-on-the-Hill and so down the winding road under tunnels of arched trees to Carsely.

James's cottage had an empty look, she noticed, and Roy suddenly said, 'Going to call on Lacey?'

'No. If you get the cases, I'll open the door.'

While Roy carried the bags in, Agatha petted her cats, who had been looked after in her absence by her cleaner, fed them and then let them out into the garden.

After they had unpacked, they settled down over coffee in the kitchen and Roy said, 'Well, let's begin. Who have we on this council?'

'For the water company, we've got Mrs Jane Cutler, Angela Buckley and Fred Shaw. Against, we've got Mr Bill Allen, Andy Stiggs, and the most vehement protester, Mary Owen. The woman whose garden the spring rises in is Robina Toynbee. We might try her first. She might have had threats. She might even know which way the late Mr Struthers was going to vote.'

'Aren't we going to eat first?'

'I'll take you to the pub.'

'None of your microwave specials?'

'I can cook now,' said Agatha defensively. 'I didn't know you were coming, so I didn't get anything in.'

When they entered the Red Lion, her eyes flew around the pub looking for James, but he was not there. 'Our Mr Lacey's taken off again,' said the landlord as he served their drinks and took their order for lunch.

'Oh,' said Agatha bleakly and then asked as casually as she could, 'Any idea where he's gone?'

'No, Mrs Darry saw him driving off.'

'How long will he be gone?'

'Nobody knows. He stopped at the shop to buy the newspapers and then he went to the police station and left his key with Fred Griggs and said he planned to be away for a bit.'

Agatha felt very low. Life had suddenly lost colour and meaning. Her fling with Guy

Freemont began to seem to her distinctly sordid.

She had again lost interest in any investigation. When they had finished their – typically English – pub meal of lasagne and chips, Agatha said, 'I'd like to go to Gerry's in Evesham first. It's that new supermarket.'

'Why?' asked Roy. 'One of the councillors work there? I thought they were all pretty well-heeled.'

'No, it's just I have no food in the house and need you to carry the bags.'

'If you must. Do you know there is a circle in hell where I will probably end up which is one huge supermarket? The shopping trolleys always go sideways, the children always scream, I always have at least one item of shopping which doesn't have the bar code on it and so I wait and wait until someone goes and finds one with the bar code and the people in the lengthening crowd behind me hate me. Or when I get to the check-out at the Express Lane, Nine Items Only, three people in front of me have at least twenty items and I haven't the courage to protest. Or the woman at the till who knows everyone in the line except me indulges in long and happy chit-chat and when it gets to me she decides to change the roll of paper in the till. Or the woman in front of me watches all her groceries sliding along and stares at them without packing them, and then she slowly takes out her cheque-book and *slowly* proceeds to write a cheque and then insists on carefully packing her plastic shopping bags according to type of grocery. And then, when it's all over and I get to the revolving doors and see daylight outside, I suddenly find myself back at the beginning of the whole process.'

'Let's go anyway,' said Agatha, who had not been listening to him.

Gerry's was jammed with shoppers. Roy suddenly decided that he would do the cooking and so proceeded to look for esoteric herbs and spices. 'Keep away from the frozen food, Aggie,' he warned. 'I can see from the gleam in your eye that you're just dying to microwave something.'

'You, for a start,' said Agatha. 'Are we ever going to get out of here?'

When they eventually got to the check-out, the trolley which, yes, slewed to one side, was piled high. The line moved forward and soon the end was in sight, only one thin woman in front of them.

'Hazel!' cried this woman to the check-out assistant. 'I didn't know you did Saturdays.'

'Need the money, Gladys,' said Hazel, one fat red hand hovering over the first item.

'Isn't that a fact,' said Gladys. 'I put in for my hip operation.'

'You'll need to wait awhile.'

'It'll be worth it. My Bert said, he said, no creature should have to endure the pain I've had. But you know what the National Health Service is like. My turn'll come round when I'm in me grave.'

'Maybe this new government . . .' began Hazel, that hand still hovering.

'Oh, get on with it!' shouted Agatha loudly.

There was a sudden silence. Agatha turned to Roy for back-up but he had disappeared. The people in the line behind her avoided eye contact.

'Well, *really*,' said Gladys. But Hazel began to slide her groceries over the scanner at great speed while Gladys began to pack, darting angry little looks at Agatha.

Gladys was at last packed and served. She threw a fulminating look at Agatha and said in a high shrill voice, 'I'm sorry for you, Hazel. If I had to deal with *some people* I would go mad.'

'Bye, Glad. Love to Bert.'

And then Hazel proceeded to open the till and change the roll of paper.

Agatha was incandescent with rage by the time she had packed up the trolley and wheeled it out to the car park as it veered crazily to the left.

Roy was waiting at the car.

'Where the hell were you?' shouted Agatha.

'I went to get cigarettes,' said Roy shiftily.

91

'You chickened out. Oh, help me get this stuff in the boot.'

They drove round Evesham's new one-way system, so hated by the traders in Bridge Street, who felt they had been left high and dry ever since it had been turned into a shopping precinct.

At last Roy said meekly, 'Are we going to Ancombe?'

'We'll take this stuff home first,' said Agatha grimly. Oh, where was James?

As they unpacked, Roy felt he could not bear the angry silence any longer and said, 'It's not my fault James has left.'

'What?'

'Well, that's why you got so shirty with that woman in the supermarket.'

'Let me tell you this. I would have got shirty with that woman in the supermarket at any time.'

'Then why take it out on me?'

'Because you're a wimp!'

'I think I may as well go back to London,' said Roy in a small voice.

'Do that!'

'I'll go and pack.'

Agatha sat down at the kitchen table and buried her face in her hands. She felt tears welling up in her eyes. Why on earth should she still get so upset over a man who showed signs of actual dislike? Perhaps, she thought, brushing the tears away, it was because of her age, because after James there might be no one left out there to love.

She got to her feet and called up the stairs. 'I'm sorry I got ratty. Want a drink?'

Roy came down the stairs, all smiles. He was an ambitious young man and did not want to offend this prickly woman whose PR skills were so admired by his boss.

'Like a drink?' repeated Agatha.

'I've given up alcohol,' said Roy, who had only drunk mineral water in the pub.

'Why?'

Roy hesitated a moment. The real reason was that it seemed to be becoming awfully fashionable *not* to drink, and Roy did not want to be out of fashion.

'Rots the brain cells, sweetie.'

'I'm going to have a stiff brandy before I go out.'

'I'd hate to see you drink alone . . .'

'I don't mind.'

'Just a teensy one, then.'

One brandy led to three and it was an amiable couple who set out for Ancombe. Agatha parked on the main road a little way along from the spring, where a group of tourists were standing staring at it and pointing. The barrier of blue-and-white police tape which had guarded the spring had been taken away.

The entrance to Robina Toynbee's cottage was by a gate in a lane which ran up the side of the cottage from the main road. 'We should have phoned first,' said Roy.

'It's all right, she's at home. She's watching us from the window.'

As Agatha raised her hand to knock at the door, Robina opened it. 'I'm delighted to see you, Mrs Raisin,' she said. 'I was thinking of phoning you to thank you. Please come in.'

The cottage was old, might even be seventeenth century, thought Agatha. The living-room was pleasant: large fireplace, low beams on the ceiling, vases of flowers, pictures and books and a cat asleep on top of the television set.

Outside the small leaded windows, a long narrow garden led down to the road, an artistic jumble of pansies, begonias, wisteria, clematis, and lobelia. There was a green lawn with a sundial next to where the spring bubbled up and then was channelled between rocks and flowers to where it disappeared through the old garden wall.

Above the fireplace was a dark oil painting of a grim old lady in an enormous cap.

'Your ancestor?' asked Agatha.

'Yes, that is Miss Jakes,' said Robina. She was wearing a soft-green velvet trouser suit. Agatha herself possessed several velvet trouser suits. She realized, looking at Robina, that velvet trouser suits were something favoured particularly by middle-aged women and decided to pack hers up and give them away to some charity shop. Although it was only late afternoon, Robina's dress was more suitable for evening. With the trouser suit, she wore sparkling ear-rings and a paste diamond necklace, and on her feet, high-heeled black satin shoes.

In the same way that some lonely women will keep a Christmas tree still lit up long after Christmas, so will they favour evening clothes during the day, as if the very sparkle and glitter could keep youth alive a little longer.

'So,' said Robina with a gentle smile, 'what will we all drink?'

'I don't know . . .' began Roy.

'Come now. That is a brandy smell, is it not? I would like to join you in a brandy.'

Agatha blinked away a picture of herself, Roy and Robina standing chatting inside a large goblet of brandy and said, yes, that would be nice.

'Here's to success,' said Robina when the drinks were served. 'I hope that is an end of the matter. So silly of them to complain about a little bit of water. I think it was all fuelled by jealousy because I am being paid by the water company. Not much, you know, but it all helps. I mean, as you must be well aware, Mrs Raisin . . .'

'Agatha.'

'Agatha. You must be aware that we have to think of our old age. These nursing homes cost a fortune.'

'I haven't begun to worry about my old age yet,' said Agatha.

'Oh, but you *should*. We can all live so dreadfully long these days.'

'I believe if you think young, you stay young.'

'So right,' said Robina, casting a flirtatious glance at Roy. 'And I am not one of those women who think having a toy boy shocking.'

'Roy is not my toy boy,' said Agatha, wondering if this gentle woman could actually be bitching her. 'So have there been any repercussions about the water deal?'

'Some very nasty threatening letters. "I'll kill you, bitch" was the last message. Anonymous, of course.'

'Did you give them to the police?'

'No, I think it is some of those environmental cranks. Do you remember when words were so simple and people talked about the countryside? There is something so threatening in the word "environment".'

'I do think you ought to tell the police about the letters,' said Agatha.

'I gather you have gained the reputation of being a bit of a *sleuth*,' said Robina. 'But there is really nothing to worry about. So much better to leave things to the experts.'

Agatha was beginning to dislike Robina.

The living-room, so pleasant when they arrived, seemed to have become claustrophobic. The day outside had suddenly darkened. Robina was wearing a very sweet, very powerful scent which mingled with the scent of some air freshener and the smell of brandy. Miss Jakes glared down at them as if to say she would not have given such people house-room in her day.

'If a murdered man had been found at the bottom of my garden and I was receiving threatening letters,' said Agatha, 'I would be very worried indeed.'

'Ah, that's because you are an incomer. Incomers never really *belong*. Us country people are so close to the soil and the violence of nature that we become tougher.'

'Us city people are so close to the violence of the streets that we have a healthy wariness,' said Agatha.

Robina waved her brandy glass and looked at Roy and raised her eyebrows. 'She doesn't understand.'

'What about the man who was murdered?' said Roy. 'Who do you think killed him?'

'That would be the Buckleys.'

'Because of the paddock?' asked Agatha.

'Oh, you've heard about that. Angela and her father are really quite coarse and brutal people.'

'So you don't think it had anything to do with the water?' asked Roy.

She gave a tinkling laugh. 'No, nothing at all. More brandy?'

'No, we must be on our way,' said Agatha, standing up. 'But please, let the police know about those letters.'

'Where to now?' asked Roy as they scampered to the car through a heavy shower of rain.

'We may as well call at the electrician's shop. We might catch Fred Shaw before he leaves.'

'Is he for or against?'

'For,' said Agatha. 'Although, after Robina, Jane Cutler and Angela, I'm beginning to think the ones against couldn't turn out to be any nastier.'

Fred Shaw was just closing up when they arrived. He hailed Agatha like an old friend and invited them into his back shop, where he opened a bottle of whisky and started to pour a strong measure in each glass.

'Here's to success,' said Fred, raising his glass. 'You sorted them out, Mrs Raisin.'

Agatha murmured, 'Success.' She covertly studied Fred Shaw. Although sixty years old, he was a powerful man with a thick neck and broad shoulders and hands.

'I only wish old Struthers was still alive,' Fred was saying.

'Why?'

'Because he was pissing about like a shy virgin over the decision. "I will give you my considered opinion all in good time." Old fart!'

'You didn't like him?'

'I should be chairman,' said Fred. 'I'd have put a bomb under this lot. Couldn't make a decision about anything to save themselves.'

'But at least Angela Buckley and Jane Cutler were on your side over the business of the water company.'

'Them! Let me tell you, Mrs Raisin, just between us, that precious pair didn't give a damn about the water company one way or t'other. They were just tired of being bossed around by Mary Owen.'

'You don't seem to like each other much in this village,' volunteered Roy.

'I've got good mates here,' said Fred, 'but none of 'em are on the council.'

'Why is that?' Roy took a good swig of whisky and mentally said goodbye to a few more brain cells. He wished he'd never been told that about dying brain cells. He could almost see the little buggers choking and gasping and expiring on a sea of whisky.

'Because this is a snobby village and we've all been councillors for yonks. Nobody stands against us. You know why? Because no one wants to take responsibility for anything these days. Why do you think we've got a Labour government in this country?'

'Because the majority of the British people voted for them,' said Agatha.

'Naw. It was because the majority of Conservative voters sat at home on their bums and didn't vote.'

'Have you any idea who might have killed Mr Struthers?' asked Roy.

Fred tapped the side of his nose. 'Let's have another.'

'I don't think . . .' Agatha began, but he was already refilling their glasses.

'Now,' said Agatha. 'Yes, cheers, Mr Shaw. You were saying?'

'There's things go on here that I know. I keep my ear to the ground. Get me?'

'Yes, yes,' said Roy, wriggling with excitement.

Fred gave him a suspicious look. 'It's a good thing I've got a dishwasher. Sterilizes things,' he said obscurely. 'Yes. Let me tell you, Peyton Place has nothing on Ancombe. Now, Mary Owen had an eye on Mr Struthers –'

'But Mr Struthers was eighty-two!'

'But Mary Owen is sixty-five, and when you get as old as that,' said Fred, just as if he weren't nearly that age himself, 'you look for security.'

'Everyone says that Mary Owen is independently wealthy!'

'Ah, but she prides herself on being a wheeler and dealer on the stock market. Believed to have lost a packet, and recently, too. So she sets her sights on old Robert Struthers. That's when our Jane Cutler moves in. Our Jane specializes in rich men who haven't long to live. It's a wonder Robert Struthers didn't die of overeating. If one of them wasn't making him meals or taking him out to dinner, the other was.'

'And who looked like winning?'

'I had my money on our Jane and Mary was fit to be tied. Council meeting two months ago, she called Jane a harlot.'

'Are you suggesting that Mary Owen murdered Mr Struthers?' asked Roy. 'Why not murder Jane Cutler?'

'Ah, that was because at that council meeting where Mary called Jane a harlot, our Robert upped and made Mary apologize. Mary said to me afterwards that Robert Struthers was a decent man who had been corrupted by Jane.'

'But murder!' protested Agatha.

'Our Mary's a powerful woman and she doesn't like anyone to get in her way.'

'All this is fascinating,' said Agatha. She could feel her head beginning to swim with all she had drunk. 'Have you told the police any of this?'

'Naw! Got no time for the police. Do you know they arrested me for drunk driving last year after I'd only had a couple of pints? Bastards. The countryside's crawling with murderers and rapists and all they can do is persecute innocent citizens. Another?'

'No, really thank you.' Agatha got to her feet. Roy was holding out his glass and she plucked it from his fingers and set it firmly on the table.

'About that fête,' said Fred. 'I'm a fine speaker.'

'I'm sure we'll find something for you,' said Agatha, now desperate to get out in the fresh air.

'That's very kind of you,' said Fred. 'I'll call on you nearer the time and we can go over my speech.'

'We can't drive, either of us,' said Agatha when they got outside. The rain had stopped and a pale washed-out evening sky stretched overhead. It had turned cold.

'Oh, come on. I'll drive,' said Roy. 'It's not far.'

'No,' said Agatha firmly. 'I've got a clean licence and it's going to stay that way and my insurance doesn't cover you driving.'

'We didn't have much to drink.'

'We did. Those glasses of whisky were enormous.'

'What about having a bash at Mary Owen?'

'Not till my head clears up. We need food. Come along, a walk will do us both good.'

They were half-way to Carsely when, against the sky pricked by the first stars, black clouds started streaming overhead.

They quickened their steps but soon the first drops began to fall and then the deluge came. By the time they finally reached Agatha's cottage, they were soaked to the skin but stone-cold sober.

After they had dried themselves and changed their clothes, Roy said he would set about making dinner, but Agatha, fearing that Roy would fuss about the kitchen, using every pot, and that they would probably end up eating at midnight, insisted on going to the pub.

When they arrived back again, she realized she had not checked her British Telecom Call Minder to see if there were any messages. The lady whose voice is on the Call Minder always seemed to Agatha an irritating relic of the days when women took elocution lessons. It was a governessy sort of eat-your-porridge-or-you-won't-go-to-the-circus sort of voice. 'Two messages,' said this voice. 'Would you like to hear them?' Did anyone *not* want to hear messages? thought Agatha crossly.

The first was from Guy Freemont. 'Been trying to get hold of you. Call me.'

The second was from Mary Owen. 'I think it is time we had a talk, Mrs Raisin. Please call me.'

Agatha looked at the clock. It was midnight. Too late to call. They had to walk back to Ancombe in the morning to pick up the car. She would see Mary Owen then.

As she fell asleep that night, her last thoughts as usual were about James. Where was he?

James, a very different-looking James, had earlier that week joined a meeting of Save Our Foxes in the back room of an Irish pub in Rugby. His black hair had been dyed blond, he had three ear-rings in one ear, and he was wearing a camouflage jacket, dirty jeans and large ex-army boots. Frightened that his accent might prove him to be an impostor, he had mostly communicated with his new companions in grunts.

He felt that if he could find out who had been paying the protesters for that demonstration at the spring, he might have a clue to the identity of the murderer.

The chairperson – stupid, stupid word, thought James with true Agatha savagery: there was either a chairman or a chairwoman, and what was wrong with that? – the chair-*thing*, then, was a thin, neurotic woman with tangled locks, a sallow, hungry face, and large, rather beautiful eyes. She was called Sybil. No one used second names. James himself had become Jim.

The purpose of this meeting was because one of the members had noticed in the local newspaper that a car salesman in Coventry was to hold a barbecue in his garden on his fortieth birthday. To celebrate his 'gypsy' heritage, he planned to serve his guests barbecued hedgehogs. A man called Trevor pointed out that hedgehogs were not a protected species, to which Sybil shouted, 'He'll find out they are now!' and got a round of applause. James covertly studied the group. They all looked militant. There was no sign of the mild-looking ones who had fronted the procession to the spring. Probably got frightened off. Nor, fortunately, was there any sign of the man who had tried to attack Agatha.

His own presence had been accepted after only one question from Sybil. How had he learned of them? Someone up in Birmingham, James had grunted.

The whole meeting was rather like a political rant. Sybil became very emotional over the plight of the hedgehogs. Why was it, James wondered, that nursery-book animals were always singled out for protection while things like spiders could be slaughtered with a free conscience?

Or if they had learned of a barn where the farmer was about to exterminate rats, would they have mustered with the same passion? And the one burning question was: Who was paying for all this? For the meeting room, for the transport to various hunts and to the spring itself?

There must be an office somewhere.

The only member who made James uneasy was a large, burly young man with a shaven head and a skull and crossbones tattooed on it. He was called Zak, and James was uncomfortably aware of Zak's eyes on him from time to time.

At last the meeting was wound up. Sybil said a bus would pick them all up in the centre of Coventry on the Saturday at 2 p.m. and take them to the wicked car salesman's barbecue.

As they were shuffling out of the door, Zak took James by the elbow in a powerful grip. 'I think we should find a place for a drink, mate,' he said.

'Got someone to see,' muttered James.

'They can wait,' said Zak, not releasing his grip on James's arm.

Not wanting to attract attention by making a scene, James allowed himself to be led out and marched along the street to another pub.

The new pub was quite respectable and fairly full. James began to relax. He could always get someone to call the police if Zak started to get nasty They ordered half-pints of bitter and took them to a corner table.

'Now, mate,' said Zak, 'what's your game?'

'What d'yer mean?' said James.

'You ain't one of them. Spotted it the minute you walked in.'

James studied Zak's unlovely face and then said in his own voice, 'Them? You said "them". Not, "one of us". What's *your* game?'

They scrutinized each other like two strange cats. James glanced under the table at Zak's feet. The torn jeans Zak was wearing ended in a pair of black lace-up shoes.

James gave a slow smile. 'Are you a detective?'

'Copper. The CID don't waste their time with a piffling thing like this. So what's your business?'

'How did you guess I wasn't one of them?'

'You're too clean and your nails are mani-cured. Did you notice the smell of unwashed bodies in there? They consider it bourgeois to wash. Sybil says that a capitalist society has removed all the exciting body odours from the British population.'

'I'm from near Ancombe,' said James. 'The village where that murder took place at the spring.'

'So what's that got to do with this lot?'

'They demonstrated at the spring. I wondered what had brought them. No animals involved.'

'You think they had something to do with the murder?'

'No, but the water company taking away the water aroused strong feelings among the members of the parish council who didn't want the water taken away. I thought one of them might have paid this lot, and if someone paid this lot, then that person might be the murderer. Who pays them, by the way? I heard somewhere that hunt saboteurs get as much as forty pounds a day.'

'Believe me, mate, that's something I've never been able to find out. You'll get paid on Saturday. Plain envelope, notes inside. We've been able to trace legitimate contributions, sad, lonely people who can only relate to animals.'

'The ones who demand unconditional love?'

'You've lost me there.'

'There's a lot of hypersensitive people around who keep getting hurt by humans and so they pour out all their love on dogs and cats, and the dogs, in particular, return the love, and they can't speak, can't nag and are not likely to run away to another owner.'

'I get it. Well, some old codger dies and either because of the reasons you gave, or because they think their relatives didn't appreciate them, they leave their money to organizations like this.'

'So do you go undercover to tip the police off when there's going to be a demonstration?'

'If it's going to be really nasty, yes, but I have to be careful. I won't bother about this thing on Saturday. If it gets rough, I'll hide behind a bush and call them in on my mobile.'

'How long have you been doing it?'

'Six months, here and there, different groups.'

'Seems a bit rough. That tattoo, for instance.'

'Washes off. Not the real thing, and my hair'll grow back in again. They've promised to take me off it soon, send someone else.'

'So is Sybil the head of this lot?'

'No. Look, they go on about the liberation of women, but these groups are as male-chauvinist-pig as you could find anywhere. So they put up some noisy female as chairperson while the fellows actually do all the organizing. You sometimes get a few upper-class ones joining in. They like a rumble for a bit of excitement and don't care what the cause is. So tell me about yourself.'

So James did: retired colonel, trying to write military history.

'I don't mind you being around and that's a fact,' said Zak when James had finished. 'But dirty up your nails a bit.'

'And you should change your shoes,' said James with a grin. 'They scream "copper".'

Car salesman Mike Pratt surveyed his appearance complacently in the mirror that Saturday. He didn't look forty. Bit of grey hair at the temples, but that gave him a distinguished look. His designer jeans had knife-edge creases and his new white leather shoes, he thought, gave him an international look. He glanced at his gold Rolex, not a real one, mind, but bought in Nathan Street in Kowloon, and who could tell the difference?

His wife came into the bedroom and stood with her thin arms folded, looking at him. Kylie was his second wife. She had been a pretty little blonde when he married her ten years ago, but now, he thought, glaring at her reflection in the mirror, she looked a fright, with dark roots showing in her blonde hair, and a skimpy T-shirt, skin-tight leggings and high-heeled shoes all accentuating her painful thinness. He tied a red scarf at the neck of his open-necked blue shirt.

'Everything's ready for you to play the big shot,' said Kylie. 'But I ain't roasting them hedgehogs, no way.'

110

'You wouldn't know how to,' sneered Mike. 'I know, just like that, cos of my gypsy background.'

'What gypsy background?' said Kylie. 'Your father's a burglar and he's still doing time.'

'I'm talking about my grandparents. My grandmother was a gypsy.' Mike took a swig of vodka from a glass on the dressing-table. His consumption of alcohol was awe-inspiring.

It is a sad trait among American alcoholics to claim a Cherokee grandmother; among their British counterparts, it is a gypsy.

Mike and Kylie Pratt lived in a neat bungalow among other neat bungalows, all almost identical with their ruched curtains at the windows and their manicured lawns.

Mike went out carrying his glass, brushing past his wife. He heard the first car arrive. He had invited all the neighbours. He was not sure how hedgehogs should be roasted, but they were meat like any other animal, and should surely simply be salted and peppered and put on the barbecue.

The day was fine, not a cloud in the sky. Feeling the lord of the manor, he advanced to meet the first of his guests.

He had paid the butcher to skin the hedgehogs, and the little carcasses lay in a pathetic bunch on a table beside the barbecue. On other tables were bowls of salads, paper plates, cups, bottles and glasses.

He felt at his best when dispensing drinks. The garden began to fill up. Voices were raised in the usual neighbourly salutations, 'You a'right? I'm a'right.' The women surrounded their men, listening eagerly as if they had not heard every word over the preceding years, prompting their spouses with little cries of 'Ye-yes. Oh, yes.'

Mike put the hedgehogs on the barbecue and poked at them with a long fork. Maybe he should have tried to cook one before. The smell was not very appetizing.

And then the protesters erupted into the garden. 'Murderer!' screamed Sybil.

Flushed with booze and outrage, Mike strode forward. 'Get out of here, you hooligans.' He punched Trevor on the arm. Trevor punched him on the nose and Mike fell back, with blood streaming down his face, while guests scattered and the television cameras whirred, for no protesters protested without informing the press of what they were about to do.

Zak crouched down behind a bush and phoned for reinforcements, which he knew were waiting in a van around the corner.

James had joined him. 'Get out there and get yourself arrested,' hissed Zak. 'I'll get you off.'

So James added to the fun by sending the barbecue flying. Burning coals rolled across the lawn.

Kylie leaned against the doorway of her house, sipping a drink, a little smile on her face. Mike's birthday was turning out to be quite fun after all.

Chapter Five

Agatha and Roy sloped around the house the next morning, both reluctant to walk even the few miles to Ancombe to tackle Mary Owen and to pick up the car.

'Let's see if there's anything on the news,' said Agatha, switching to Sky Television.

'It's not on the hour,' complained Roy. 'It's eleven-twenty and it's all that dreary sports.'

'Only last for ten minutes,' said Agatha, sitting down in front of the set clutching a cup of coffee.

'There won't be anything about the murder,' said Roy.

'Let's see.'

The sports finished, then the ads. Then both sat up straight as the news came on again and a voice said, 'The barbecue of a Mr Mike Pratt of Coventry was the subject of attack yesterday by members of Save Our Foxes.'

'It's them,' said Agatha eagerly.

The voice went on to explain about the barbecuing of the hedgehogs. 'Look at that blazing sunshine,' complained Roy. 'You'd think Coventry was at the other end of the earth instead of being in the Midlands like us. Why did we have to get soaked?'

'Shh!' hissed Agatha.

A blond man with an ugly sneer on his face was pushing the barbecue over. Agatha stiffened. 'Doesn't that chap look like James?'

'You poor thing.' Roy shook his head. 'You're beginning to see Lacey everywhere. Let's go. At least the Coventry sunshine has reached us.'

'Isn't this beautiful?' said Roy as he trotted along by Agatha's side on the road to Ancombe.

Agatha grunted by way of reply, but wondering again why the sheer beauty of the spring countryside did not seem to get *inside* her. She remembered passing some Saturdays of her underprivileged childhood at the art gallery in Birmingham studying English landscapes, enjoying the painted scenery which had become part of that early dream of living in the countryside one day. And so she saw the present passing landscape like a painting. That bright green of the new leaves, she'd had that colour in her art class at school. And the curved furrows of a ploughed field, with the trees at the edge raising their branches to the blue sky, looked like one of those paintings. Perhaps one had to be brought up in the country to really appreciate it.

'Do you believe in God?' asked Roy suddenly.

'Don't know,' said Agatha, wondering if the person in the sky with whom she frequently made bargains – get me out of this one and I'll give up smoking – really did exist.

'I believe in Nature,' said Roy, spreading his arms wide. 'That's what it's all about.'

'You're not going to start hugging trees?' said Agatha suspiciously. 'I've got to live here.'

'I'm trying to explain I'm a pagan,' said Roy. 'I am as one with all this.'

Agatha was about to say something waspish, but Roy's thin, weak face was turned up to the sun and he looked supremely happy. 'Glad you're enjoying yourself,' she said gruffly.

'Funny,' said Roy, taking her arm, 'I always thought anyone who moved out of the city was mad, but maybe if I lowered my sights, it would be better. You and me, Aggie, we could team up and start a new agency in Mircester. Do local accounts. Maybe get married.'

'And spend my declining years with people mistaking you for my son?'

'Think about it. We get on all right.'

Agatha privately thought that a very little of Roy went a long way, but she gently detached her arm and said, 'Okay, I'll think about it.' Then she said, 'Do we really have to go on with this? It's funny how people in villages so close by can be so different. Apart from the dreadful Mrs Darry and a few others, the people in Carsely are wonderful. But the ones we've met in Ancombe seem to be really nasty, and Mary Owen is surely going to be the nastiest of all.'

'You've dealt with nasty people all your life, Aggie.'

True, thought Agatha, and it used to be all the same to me, nice or nasty, just a job, but now I've learned to like people.

'Where does Mary Owen live?' she realized Roy was asking.

'I looked her up. She lives in Ancombe Manor, far end of the village. We'll pick up the car and drive.'

Soon they were turning in at the entrance to the manor. Thick yew hedges lined either side of the narrow drive, giving Agatha the impression of driving through a maze. Suddenly they were in front of the house. It was old, very old, made of Cotswold stone, rambling and covered in ivy. It looked as if it had been there so long that it had become part of the surrounding countryside.

Agatha's sharp eyes noticed that there were weeds sprouting in the gravel-covered circle outside the manor-house. She began to think the report that Mary Owen had fallen on hard times might be true. Such a house would have housed an army of indoor and outdoor servants in the old days.

'Well, here goes for another barrage of insults,' said Agatha, pushing an anachronistic bell-push by the side of the iron-studded door.

At first they thought there was no one at home, but then they heard footsteps approaching.

The door opened. Mary Owen stood there. She was wearing a shabby sweater and stained riding-breeches and boots. Her head was tied up in a scarf and she held a duster in one hand.

Her contemptuous eyes raked them.

'What do you want?'

'I am Agatha Raisin –'

'I know that. And who's your creature?'

'This is Mr Roy Silver,' said Agatha firmly, thinking if one was prepared for insult, it certainly helped one not to lose one's temper.

'Out with it, then. Haven't you done enough damage, whoring for that damned water company?'

Roy timidly tugged at Agatha's arm, but Agatha smiled pleasantly. 'I just wanted to talk to you.'

'About what?'

'The murder.'

Mary stood scowling at the duster in her hand. Then she jerked her head. 'Come in.'

They followed her into a small dark hall and then along a stone-flagged corridor to a kitchen. 'Sit down,' barked Mary. They sat down at the kitchen table. Mary jerked out a chair with the toe of one boot and sat down facing them.

'You have a bit of a reputation as a detective,' said Mary.

'I have solved some cases,' said Agatha.

'So you say. The only reason I'm bothering with you is that you might get the police to see some sense. You see, I know who murdered Robert Struthers.'

'Who?' demanded Agatha and Roy in unison.

'Jane Cutler, that's who!'

'Why?' asked Agatha. 'I heard she hoped to marry him.'

'Of course she did. That ghoul specializes in marrying men who are due to drop dead, only Robert didn't have terminal cancer or anything like that. He could have lived to a hundred. So she helped him on his way.'

'But what good would that do her?' Agatha looked every bit as bewildered as she felt.

'Because I believe she talked poor Robert into making out his will in her favour.'

120

'But you don't know for sure!'

'I know. Do me a favour and get it out of your police friends. Now if you don't mind, I have work to do.'

'So what do you think of that?' asked Roy as they drove off.

'I think we should drive to Mircester and see what we can get out of Bill Wong.'

'Why do you think she sneered at me like that?' demanded Roy moodily. 'Creature, indeed.'

'She was furious with me and you just happened to be there.'

Roy's thin face lightened. 'That's it. It can't be my clothes. I mean, this sweater's Italian and cost a mint, and my jeans are stone-washed.'

Agatha privately thought that no matter how much money he spent on clothes, Roy would always look somehow as if he belonged in one of those London street gangs of white-faced undernourished youths.

'Oh, bugger,' said Agatha as they drove into Mircester. 'Market-day. No central parking, and I'm sick of walking.'

'Park right there!' said Roy.

'It's a yellow line. No parking.'

'Just park,' said Roy, fumbling in his back pocket and taking out his wallet. He fished out a 'disabled' sticker and affixed it on Agatha's windscreen.

'Where did you get that?'

'From a friend,' said Roy.

'But what if some copper comes along?'

'We can always drool at the mouth and say we're mentally disabled. Come along.'

They went into the police headquarters and asked for Bill Wong. 'We should have phoned,' said Agatha, as they waited. 'He's probably out.'

But after a few minutes, Bill appeared.

'I hope you've got something for me,' he said. 'I'm busy.' He led the way to an interviewing-room.

Agatha outlined everything she had learned since the last time she had seen him, ending up with Mary Owen's claim that Jane Cutler had murdered Robert Struthers to inherit after his death.

'Not the case,' said Bill. 'His son gets everything, not even a mention of either Jane Cutler or Mary Owen in the will.'

'Oh,' said Agatha, disappointed.

'This old boy, I mean Struthers,' said Roy, 'could have been playing both of them along. Old people sometimes do that to get attention. I mean, he liked playing cagey. He wouldn't tell any of the other councillors which way he meant to vote. Strikes me as being manipulative and liking his little bit of power. Just suppose Jane Cutler thought she was in the will.'

'That's a good point,' said Bill, 'but why not get him to marry her and be absolutely sure? Common sense would tell her that he would leave it all to his son. Then Jane Cutler is rich, and if Mary Owen has fallen on hard times, and *she* believed he had changed his will in *her* favour, then she might have bumped him off and then accused Jane to deflect any suspicions from her, although it's all very far-fetched.'

'James has disappeared,' said Agatha. 'Have you heard anything?'

Yes, Bill had through the grapevine learned that James was masquerading as a member of Save Our Foxes, but he didn't want to tell Agatha that. He felt the less Agatha saw of James, the better. Out of sight was out of mind.

'No,' he lied. 'Probably off on his travels.'

Agatha pulled herself together. 'You said they had decided that Struthers had been killed elsewhere and dumped at the spring. Any forensic evidence?'

'Nothing much. Forensic believes that some-one vacuumed the body before dumping it. There was just one thing. A white cat hair in one of his turn-ups. He wore those old-fashioned trousers.'

Agatha's eyes gleamed. 'So we are looking for someone with a white cat!'

'Do you know, there isn't one white cat in the village of Ancombe?' said Bill. 'We went from house to house. Someone could be lying, of course.'

'It needn't be an all-white cat,' said Roy. 'Could be one of those black-and-white things.'

'Sorry. I should have explained that the hair was from a Persian cat.'

'Definitely a Persian, and a cat?' asked Agatha. 'It couldn't have been a dog?'

Agatha would have loved it to turn out to have been Mrs Darry.

'Definitely a Persian cat.'

'Still, it's something to go on,' said Agatha eagerly.

'I don't want to dampen your enthusiasm for amateur detection, but a great number of policemen have been searching for that cat and are still searching.'

'Does Mary Owen have an alibi?'

'Yes, on the night of the murder she was staying with her sister in Mircester. She stayed all night.'

'But he could have been killed earlier in the day!'

'It's always hard to estimate time of death, but he was killed earlier that evening. Mary

Owen's sister said she arrived at four in the afternoon and did not leave until the following morning.'

'A sister would say anything.'

'True, but she seems a very direct, truthful sort of lady. Now, I've really got to get back to work.'

As Agatha and Roy approached Agatha's car, a large policeman was standing staring at it.

'Limp!' hissed Roy.

The policeman swung round and watched their approach. 'Thank you, dear boy,' quavered Agatha. 'I am getting so forgetful. I cannot remember where I left my stick.'

Hoping desperately it was not some policeman who had seen her before, Agatha smiled at him weakly and allowed Roy to help her into the driving seat. As soon as Roy was in behind her, she drove off with a great grinding and clashing of gears.

'Okay, I'm nervous,' said Agatha. 'The minute we stop I'm going to get that sticker off the windscreen.'

'Where now?'

'Let's go back to Ancombe and have a wander around. We might see that cat.'

'We haven't eaten and I'm starving.'

'We'll eat in the pub in Ancombe.'

'What about all that food I was going to

cook? I've got to get the London train this evening.'

'Next time,' said Agatha.

James and Zak had agreed not to be seen spending too much time together. There was a member of Save Our Foxes called Billy Guide who drank heavily. James targeted him, buying the grateful Billy as much as he could drink.

A week after Agatha's interview with Mary Owen, James attended another meeting and his heart beat faster when he learned that the group's next expedition was to the spring in Ancombe.

Sybil, her fine eyes flashing, said they would take bags of cement and put them into the basin of the spring.

James, who longed to point out that their plan would cause more destruction to the village environment than the water company, kept silent. Why should such a group switch their attention from animals to the matter of spring water? Someone must be paying them for this action. Sybil was saying that the bus would pick them up at the usual place.

He half-listened to her rant, wondering if she believed a word of it.

Various other members made rousing speeches. James stifled a yawn. He roused himself when he heard Trevor ask if the press had been informed.

'No,' said Sybil. 'When the spring is cemented up, we'll phone them.'

'Wait a bit,' slurred Billy Guide, 'if the basin is filled with cement, that means the water from the spring will flood that woman's garden – what's her name? – Toynbee.'

'And serve her right!' cried Sybil. 'It's all her fault that capitalist commercialism has been allowed to pollute one of our English villages.'

At last the meeting finished. James edged up to Billy. 'Fancy a drink?'

'Okay, squire,' said Billy, 'but I'm a bit broke.'

'On me.'

'Great.'

'Let's find a pub a bit away from here,' said James, knowing that Billy would go anywhere for a free drink.

On the road to the pub, Billy said, 'My missus is always complaining I come home smelling of beer.'

'Let's have vodka,' said James. 'That doesn't smell.'

And may God forgive me, he thought. I didn't think any of this useless lot were married. Billy already smelt like a brewery, but James was only interested in getting him drunk enough to loosen up.

He didn't, however, want Billy to get so drunk that he couldn't think or speak.

'Have you been married long?' he asked.

'Ten years.'

'Kids?'

'Four.'

'You haven't got a job, have you? What do you live on?'

'Missus goes out cleaning and the mother-in-law takes care of the kids.'

So much for women's liberation, thought James bleakly.

Billy went into a long rambling monologue about the unfairness of life.

At last James asked, 'How did you get into this Save Our Foxes business?'

'Get a bit o' drink money.'

'Do you care about saving foxes?'

Billy gave him a sly grin. 'O' course. Got to save the little bleeders.'

'What I can't understand,' said James, 'is why you're all so interested in this spring? Who's paying you?'

'You know, Jim. We go along. Have a bit of a punch-up. Get forty quid. Not bad.'

'But, I mean, where does the money come from to pay us?'

'We're not supposed to know, Jim. But I heard . . .'

Billy looked thoughtfully down at his empty glass.

'I'll get us another,' said James quickly.

He returned with two vodkas. Billy was never quite drunk, never quite sober. He seemed to be able to sink an enormous capacity without falling over. James was beginning to feel pretty drunk himself, and he was anxious to get some facts out of Billy while he was still able to.

'You were saying about who was paying us?' asked James.

'Was I?' Billy looked suddenly truculent and suspicious. 'What's a posh fellow like you doing with us lot?' James had given up trying to hide his accent.

'Because a bit of a punch-up is fun,' he said.

'That's what I thought.' Billy raised his glass. 'Here's to you.'

'So I mean, who's paying? Not to mention paying fines for disturbance of the peace?'

Billy leaned forward. 'Sybil and Trevor like to keep us in the dark about that. Playing at spies, like. But I heard Sybil say something like, I got the money from that Owen woman.'

Mary Owen. I'll be damned, thought James, masking his excitement.

To his relief he heard the barman call, 'Time, gennelmun, pullease.' Got the information just in the nick of time.

He said goodbye to Billy outside the pub and hurried back to his temporary room. He

129

would hang around a few days to allay suspicion and then he would head back to Carsely and call Bill Wong to tell him he had solved the murder. For if Mary Owen felt so passionately about the spring, then it followed that she must have committed the murder. And James wanted Agatha to be there when he told Bill.

He thought briefly of Zak. Perhaps he should tell Zak – but then James wanted all the glory for himself.

James returned to Carsely early in the morning on the day before the attack on the spring was due to take place.

He phoned Bill Wong and asked him to call at ten in the morning. No, he couldn't tell him over the phone. It was only fair that Agatha should hear his news at the same time.

He decided to walk next door to Agatha's cottage and give her the invitation. He felt quite like Poirot and only wished he had a library so that he could stand on the hearthrug in front of the marble fireplace and tell them how it had all been done.

But as soon as he stepped outside his own front door he saw a car parked behind Agatha's, outside her front door.

That chap from the water company. And James was willing to bet he hadn't been making an early-morning call but had stayed the night.

Muzzy with sex and sleep, Agatha awoke to the shrill sound of the telephone ringing.

She grabbed the receiver.

'Agatha!' It was James.

'Yes?'

'I have something to tell you and Bill Wong about the murder. Can you be at my cottage at ten this morning?'

'Yes.'

'Goodbye.'

'Who was that?' demanded Guy, stretching and yawning.

'Just a neighbour,' said Agatha. 'Got to get dressed.'

She went through to the bathroom and leaned on the wash-hand basin and stared at her puffy face and tousled hair in the mirror. When she was young, a night of love-making would leave her looking radiant. Now that she was old, it seemed to do nothing but accentuate the bags under the eyes and the lines down either side of the mouth.

What did James want? And why, oh why, had he chosen this morning of all mornings to phone?

She washed and dressed, made up with care, and went down to the kitchen, where Guy was sitting at the table in one of her frilly dressing-gowns drinking coffee.

He gave her a warm smile. Agatha blinked at him. She wished she had never gone to bed

131

with him again. But James seemed to have been gone so long and they had both drunk rather a lot at dinner the night before.

She wondered if Guy felt any affection for her at all. Charles, that wretched baronet, had seemed to treat her as an easy lay, but he had teased her and laughed at her and had seemed genuinely fond of her in his way. But Guy seemed to be acting a part.

Agatha glanced at the kitchen clock. Five minutes to ten. 'I've got to go,' she said hurriedly 'Could you let yourself out? And won't you be in trouble turning up late at the office?'

He laughed. 'One of the benefits of being a director is one can turn up late at the office.'

She bent over him and gave him a peck on the cheek. 'Phone you later,' said Agatha and made her escape.

It had been raining during the night and the air was fresh and clean, making Agatha feel soiled and depraved. She hoped to have a few words with James, but when she arrived outside his door she was joined by Bill Wong, who had just driven up.

Bill and Agatha stared in amazement at the blond and ear-ringed James who answered the door.

'What's happened to you?' asked Agatha.

'Part of my disguise,' said James. 'I've been undercover. Come in and sit down and I'll tell you who murdered Robert Struthers.'

'So you've been investigating on your own.' Colour flamed in Agatha's face.

'You've got a love-bite on your neck,' said James coldly.

'Here, now,' admonished Bill. 'This is important.'

They all sat down, Agatha and Bill on a sofa facing James, who sat in his favourite armchair.

'I joined Save Our Foxes,' said James.

'So it *was* you I saw on television,' cried Agatha.

'The barbecue? Yes, that was me,' said James proudly. 'Well, here's what I found out. They are going to the spring tomorrow afternoon and they are going to block it off with cement. And that's not all. I've found out who's paying them to demonstrate. Mary Owen.'

'But according to gossip, she's fallen on hard times,' said Agatha. 'So she couldn't afford to pay them.'

'The gossip, like most village gossip, is probably wrong,' said James loftily. 'Anyone who can pay this bunch of thugs to behave badly must have felt passionately enough about the whole affair to have murdered Struthers.'

Agatha was suddenly glad of James's horribly bleached hair and ear-rings. It was easy to think of him as a stranger. She suddenly felt very tired. All she hoped was that Guy had taken himself off so that she could creep back under the duvet and go to sleep.

'Did you report this to Zak?' asked Bill sharply.

'Who's Zak?' asked Agatha.

'An undercover policeman who made himself known to James.'

Both looked at James. 'I hadn't time to get to him.'

'We know from him about the protest tomorrow,' said Bill.

'So you knew where James was all along,' said Agatha furiously, glaring at Bill.

'But Zak didn't know about Mary Owen,' said James quickly. 'I found that out by getting one of the members drunk.'

'We'll pull her in for questioning. She has an alibi,' said Bill. 'On the night of the murder she was staying with her sister in Mircester.'

'Her sister could be covering for her.'

'You haven't met the sister, a Mrs Darcy, straight-talking, honest. But we'll check out the alibi again.'

'You should have told me about this, James,' said Agatha. 'We've always investigated things together in the past.'

'I would have done if you hadn't been preoccupied in screwing around with a toy boy.'

'That's enough.' Bill got to his feet. 'Come along, Agatha.'

When they had gone, James phoned a hair-dresser in Evesham and made an appointment to get his hair dyed back to its normal colour. Agatha and Bill had made him feel small and petty. Bill was right. He should have told Zak.

When Agatha went into her cottage, her phone was ringing. She answered it and found it was Roy Silver.

'Just calling to see how things are going,' he said cheerfully.

'Murder or water?'

'Murder.'

Agatha told him about James. Roy listened and then said, 'That was a bit mean of him.'

She warmed to him. 'Why not come down for the weekend and we'll go and watch the demonstration?'

'Great. I'll get the early-morning train.'

Agatha put down the phone feeling better. However outrageously Roy had behaved in the past, he always popped up again and she felt like company. She remembered Guy and swore under her breath. She had been so stunned after leaving James that she had not even checked to see if his car was still outside.

'Guy!' she called up the stairs.

There was no reply. With a little sigh of relief, she went up and stripped the bed and put on a clean sheet, pillow cases and duvet cover. Then she undressed and climbed into bed and plunged down immediately into a dreamless sleep. An hour later, she could faintly hear the phone downstairs ringing. She had switched off the one in the bedroom. She lay until it had finished ringing and then went back to sleep.

In the cottage next door, James replaced the receiver. He had planned to ask Agatha to come into Evesham with him, but he rang off the minute her answering service came on the line.

Rain was thudding down on to the platform at Moreton-in-Marsh Station next morning as Agatha waited for the arrival of Roy Silver.

A large bouquet of flowers from Guy had arrived just before she left. She had slung them into a bucket of water, planning to arrange them later. She wondered why the idea of having a handsome man send her flowers was so infinitely depressing.

The Great Western train slid smoothly alongside the platform. Roy appeared looking quite ordinary for once in a Burberry worn over cords and a sports shirt and V-necked sweater.

'Hello, Aggie,' he said, planting a wet kiss on her cheek. 'I hope we don't get this weather for the fête. What will we do?'

'I've already contacted one of those firms that rent out marquees. They'll have to be decorated and some heat supplied. There's nothing more dampening than people crowded into damp tents with the rain pouring down. The Freemonts were all for having an orchestra, but I persuaded them that the Carsely village band would be more traditional. They're actually jolly good. Don't want to make it too ritzy. When it's good weather here, I always envisage the fête being held on a cloudless day, but when it's like this, I picture it as being damp and horrible and full of crying children.'

'We'll see,' said Roy. 'How could we find out if Mary Owen has money or not?'

'We could ask Angela Buckley. She's pretty direct, although, come to think of it, she did warn me off.'

'Now why did she warn you off? She must have something to hide. Let's go and see her.'

'All right. We'll leave your bags first and have a coffee.'

After Roy had taken his bag up to the spare room, he joined Agatha in the kitchen.

He looked at the flowers in the bucket, and then picked up the florist's card which Agatha had left on the table. 'Oho,' said Roy. '"Love from Guy." That wouldn't be the delicious Guy Freemont, would it?'

'We have a close working arrangement,' said Agatha frostily.

'If you say so, dear.' He accepted a mug of coffee. 'So after we see this Angela, I suppose we go to the spring for a punch-up. I wonder if Mary Owen really has money. What about asking James?'

'No.'

'Have it your way. Is that sunlight outside?'

Agatha walked to the window and looked out. Raindrops glistened on the bushes and flowers in the garden. 'I'll be able to let the cats out,' she said, opening the door. Hodge and Boswell slid through and disappeared into the shrubbery.

'I could fix up a cat flap for you,' said Roy. 'I'm pretty good at DIY.'

'I never got around to getting one. I keep imagining some small, slim burglar crawling through it at night.'

'Have it your way.'

Half an hour later, they set out for Ancombe, driving through the glittering rain-washed countryside. Agatha opened the car windows. The air was heavy with the scent of flowers.

She drove through puddles, sending up sheets of water on either side of the car. Roy began to sing happily in a flat, reedy voice. 'I'm not very good at leisure,' said Agatha.

Roy stopped singing. 'How come?'

'I was just thinking that on a day like this, I should be sitting in the garden with my cats, reading or just looking. I always seem to be *doing* something. If I'm idle, I feel guilty.'

'Take up a sport, then, tennis or something. Good for the waistline. Is that a bite on your neck, Aggie?'

'Insect bite.'

'Oh, yes? I know those sort of insects. We have them in London as well.'

'Here's Ancombe,' said Agatha, anxious to change the subject. 'The Buckley farm is off this way.'

Soon they were bumping up the farm drive. 'Looks prosperous,' said Roy.

'Never can tell with farmers, I gather,' said Agatha. 'They can't all have that rich or idyllic a life, or so many of them wouldn't commit suicide.'

'It's all those things they do with animals. I don't think so many people are eating meat. *I* don't. And I read that nobody wants to eat pork. They eat bacon, but no pork chops.'

'I'll tell you why that is. When did you last have a pork chop that tasted like anything? You're not thinking of joining an animal-rights group, are you?'

'Not me, sweetie. I just don't enjoy meat so much. Feels unhealthy.'

'Here we are.' Agatha drew up outside the farm door. 'And there is Angela.'

Angela Buckley stood watching them, strong arms folded across a checked shirt-covered bosom, strong legs in cord and cowboy boots.

'Wouldn't want to meet her on a dark night,' muttered Roy.

They got out of the car. Agatha introduced Roy.

'What d'you want?' demanded Angela harshly. 'Not still poking your nose into things that are none of your business, are you?'

'Did you know Mary Owen was paying those Save Our Foxes people to demonstrate, and that they're going to be at the spring this afternoon to fill it in with cement?'

'What? You'd better come indoors. I've got the kettle on.'

'I like this,' said Roy, looking around the farm kitchen. 'So truly rural.'

Angela flashed him a look of contempt.

'So what's this about Mary?' She took the kettle off the Aga and proceeded to make a pot of coffee.

Roy watched anxiously. Angela's way of making coffee consisted of spooning coffee into the pot and pouring boiling water on top of it. He hoped she would allow the grounds to settle, but she stirred the mixture up with a long spoon. Agatha said black and Roy, white, and then Roy bleakly looked down at the gritty coffee swirling around in his cup.

140

Agatha explained again about Mary. 'The old bitch,' said Angela furiously. 'I hope the police have arrested her.'

'They've taken her in,' said Agatha. 'But what puzzles me is that Fred Shaw said Mary was broke and that's why she wanted to marry Robert Struthers. But if she's broke, how come she could pay these people – wages, transport, not to mention bags of cement, and fines in court?'

'I think Fred Shaw invented the whole thing. He's always sneering because Mary lives in the manor and doesn't seem to put much money into it. She does all the cleaning herself, things like that. Did he say Mary wanted to marry old Robert?'

'Yes, and he said Jane Cutler was after him as well.'

Angela's face darkened. 'That I could believe. The mercenary old bag.'

'Don't you think Mary could have murdered Struthers? She must have felt very strongly about the spring to pay Save Our Foxes.' Agatha took out a tissue and dabbed at the moustache of coffee grounds above her mouth.

'She felt very strongly about having her will crossed. I noticed she always seemed to be wining and dining Robert, but I thought that was because she didn't like not getting her own way and Robert used to drive her mad

141

with exasperation because he wouldn't tell her of his decision.'

'Why did you warn me off?'

'Because,' said Angela patiently, 'once you start digging around people's personal lives, a lot of people get hurt, and unnecessarily so.' She glared at Roy. 'Who the hell are you?'

'Friend of Aggie's down for the weekend. Me and Aggie go back a long way.'

'You're too young to go back a long way. You don't have to try to make a liaison look respectable to me.'

'Oh, for Pete's sake,' howled Agatha. 'Can't I have a conversation with anyone in this damn village without being insulted?'

'If you poke around people's private lives to find out the worst about them, they're bound to think the worst of you,' said Angela. 'Now, I'm busy. Why don't you push off?'

'Well!' said Roy when they drove off. 'Is it something in the soil here that makes everyone bitter and twisted? Feel like seeing anyone else?'

Agatha looked at the clock on the dashboard. 'No, let's have lunch, and then go to the spring for the fun and games.'

As they sat over lunch, Roy asked if anything had been found out about the cat with white hair. 'Not that I know of,' said Agatha. 'You remember, we looked and looked.'

They heard the wail of police sirens in the distance. 'The troops have arrived,' said Roy. 'Cheer up, Aggie. All this will keep Ancombe in the news.'

They left the car outside the pub and walked along to the spring. Alerted by the sirens, villagers were starting to make their way along as well.

Agatha saw Bill Wong talking to some policemen and went across to him. He led her a little to one side. 'Mary Owen does have a cast-iron alibi.'

'But her sister could be covering for her, surely?'

'She was seen by the neighbours. The curtains in the evening weren't drawn and the two sisters could be seen sitting over dinner, and talking.'

'Rats. Back to square one. Have you arrested Mary Owen?'

'No, there's nothing illegal about donating money to these groups. Unless we can get one of them to confess that Mary Owen actually told them to take action, we haven't anything on her. And she says all that about her being broke is a fiction and says we can check with her bank.'

'What about that chap who told James she was paying them?'

'Billy Guide? With any luck he'll be with the rest. Here's James.'

James and Agatha exchanged frosty little nods.

'Here come the protesters,' said Roy.

The bus carrying them stopped a little way along the road. Agatha could see several of them glaring out at the unexpected sight of the large police presence. They argued for a few minutes, then the door of the bus slid open. Four of the men appeared, carrying between them a bag of cement.

Followed by the others, they headed for the spring. James, his hair dyed back to its normal colour and minus the ear-rings, said to Bill Wong, 'Billy Guide is not among them, and where's Zak?'

'He was pulled out. After seeing us all here today, they'd start searching around for an informer. They'll probably think it was you, but they might have picked on Zak, and he was fed up with the job anyway. Billy Guide was taken to hospital the day after your hospitality suffering from pancreatitis.'

A policeman stood in front of the four carrying the bag of cement. 'Where are you going with that?'

'Keep going!' shouted Sybil from behind them. 'Don't let the pigs stop you.'

To the protesters' surprise, the policeman stood aside. They marched to the spring and one slit open the neck of the bag of cement.

That, of course, Agatha realized, was the moment the police had been waiting for. They had to be caught in the act of trying to block the spring. The men were seized, the bag wrenched away. The other protesters, about twenty of them, began attacking the police, kicking and punching and gouging.

Sybil was dragged past James by two policemen. She looked at him as she passed with dawning recognition and then spat full in his face.

'I quite warm to that girl,' said Agatha.

Chapter Six

Agatha went back to London with Roy after the weekend. She knew journalists, ever fickle creatures, were quite capable of forgetting to turn up for the fête, and needed to be reminded of it and bullied all over again into coming. She also needed an excuse to get away from Carsely, James and Guy.

At first she found the journalists had become lukewarm about the prospect of a visit down to the country to a fête to celebrate the launch of water, of all things. So Agatha told them all about the attempt to block up the spring, which the television stations and national newspapers had heard about too late to film or photograph. Agatha hinted darkly at fears of an almighty punch-up on the day of the fête, painting an alarming picture of sweet little children sent flying by protesters, and village ladies screaming in fright. Interest in the fête was reanimated to such an extent that Agatha thought at times it might be a good idea to pay the protesters herself to turn up.

By the end of her week, she felt she had done very well, only to receive a set-back just as she was preparing to leave. Jane Harris, the film star who was to open the fête, would not attend. Her agent phoned to say that Ms Harris had read the reports of the murder at Ancombe and the demonstrations and she sympathized with the demonstrators, as she considered English rural life should be protected.

'The silly bitch lives between Chelsea and L.A.,' howled Agatha.

The agent hung up on her.

I'm losing my touch, thought Agatha miserably. Now who do I get? It had better be someone good or the Freemonts will be cancelling my contract.

The phone rang. It was Mrs Bloxby, the vicar's wife. 'How did you get my number?' asked Agatha.

'You left it with me, don't you remember? How are things?'

'Not very well. I have to stay on. Jane Harris has cancelled. I haven't told the water company yet. I need to get a replacement.'

There was a long silence.

'Are you still there?' Agatha demanded.

'I'm thinking.'

Agatha sighed. She was very fond of the vicar's wife, but how on earth could she help?

148

'I have it,' said Mrs Bloxby.

'What?' asked Agatha.

'The Pretty Girls.'

'Who are they when they're at home?'

Mrs Bloxby laughed. 'I never expected to be more up in the world than you. They are a pop group. Number one on the hit parade. They are a new type of pop singer. Very pretty, and wear old-fashioned clothes. They do a lot for charity. Who gets the money from the fête?'

'The water company, I suppose.'

'If you say the money is going to help AIDS – The Pretty Girls support that – I think if they are free, they would do it. They would be a big crowd-puller. They also support animal liberation, so their presence at the fête will give it respectability with environmental groups.'

'You're a genius,' said Agatha. 'I'll get on to it right away.'

Some hard phoning later and Agatha to her delight had secured the presence of The Pretty Girls. She then phoned the water company in Mircester and was put through to Peter Freemont.

'I don't think Jane Harris is the right person,' said Agatha, proceeding to lie. She felt that Jane Harris turning down the fête reflected badly on her business abilities. 'So I secured The Pretty Girls.'

'You're brilliant, Agatha. How on earth did you get them to come?'

149

'We'll contribute the money from the fête to AIDS.'

'After deductions for the costs?'

'Of course.'

'I just don't know how you do it. They're number one on the hit parade.'

'I know.' Agatha felt uncomfortable at not giving Mrs Bloxby any credit for the idea, but it was a hard world and she did not want to admit she had never heard of the pop group, Agatha's interest in pop groups having stopped when she retired and gave up representing some of them.

She found out afterwards that The Pretty Girls had risen to fame in one meteoric month and felt better about being so behind the times. She then stayed on in London anyway to make the rounds with this new information, this time choosing journalists from the entertainment pages.

Agatha had also secured the attendance of old Lord Pendlebury, a local peer, to give away the prizes at a children's talent competition.

By the time she travelled back to Carsely, she felt she was on the brink of pulling off the biggest public relations coup of her career.

The weather in July was perfect, one sunny day following another. Agatha kept herself busy. She had resolved to end the affair with

Guy, but each cold, hard look from James, when she crossed his path, sent her straight back into Guy's ever-ready company. She hated the age difference. She had completed her delayed appointments with the beautician, and still felt all the strain of keeping up appearances. She found she kept studying women of her own age, anxious to avoid wearing the sort of clothes that middle-aged women wore, such as the aforementioned velvet trouser suits. In fact, decided Agatha, unless the middle-aged figure was slim and youthful-looking, all trouser suits were out. And those striped French sailor sweaters. Sign of a skittish, middle-aged woman. Noel Coward's Mrs Wentworth-Brewster.

But at least all the worries about ageing and all the arrangements for the fête kept her very busy and James was centred somewhere deep inside her, a little dark ache, but nothing more.

The golden days moved into August. Murder and the non-existence of a white Persian cat were forgotten. There were no more anti-spring demonstrations.

Finally it was the eve of the fête. Agatha returned with Roy from patrolling the site, checking the marquees, going over all the arrangements. The weather forecast was doubtful. Showers were expected but not due to arrive until the following evening, when the fête would be all over.

Agatha and Roy sat out in the garden of her cottage with tall, cold drinks. 'Anyone been trying to get hold of you?' asked Roy lazily.

'I'd better go in and check the Call Minder,' said Agatha. 'In a minute.'

'So you and James are definitely finished?'

'It was all over a long time ago. I don't want to talk about it. I'll go and check for messages.'

Agatha went in and dialled her code. How many times had she dialled those digits, hoping to hear a message from James. 'You have three messages,' said the prissy voice. 'Do you want to hear them?'

'Yes,' said Agatha. It was no use shouting, 'Of course I want to hear them, you stupid bitch,' because the computer rejected insults.

The first message was from Robina Toynbee. She sounded strained. 'Please phone me, Mrs Raisin. It is very important.'

The second message was from Portia, the Freemonts's elegant secretary. She did not like Agatha and her voice was thin and cold. 'Please liaise with Mr Peter at the management tent at nine a.m.'

The third message was from The Pretty Girls' agent. 'Disaster, isn't it? Of course they won't be there. Can you believe it? How could they destroy success just like that?'

Agatha looked up the agent's office number, but got the 'engaged' signal. She called to Roy. 'I can't make head or tail of a message from

Carol, The Pretty Girls' agent, and her line's engaged. She says they won't be there and they've destroyed their success.'

'Put on the television. It's near the hour.'

Agatha put on Sky, and they sat down in front of it, both of them with their backs rigid and their eyes staring at the screen.

It was the very first news item. Police had raided a house in Fulham where The Pretty Girls had been giving a party and had seized large quantities of Ecstasy, heroin, uppers and pot. Pretty Girl Sue, the leader of the group, had been found stuffed in a cupboard, unconscious from an overdose. Then followed a brief history of the pop group, whose fame had been built up on their clean family image.

'What'll we do?' said Agatha, her face white. 'We can't get anyone else at this late date.'

'We're stuck with Lord Pendlebury,' said Roy.

'But don't you see what this means?' howled Agatha. 'The press will not turn up, not the nationals, only the locals. I didn't bother a last-minute chase-up of the press because of The Pretty Girls. We'd better start now. What do I say?'

'Christ knows,' said Roy. 'Hint at another murder. Hint at a demonstration.'

Agatha began to phone up every newspaper and television station. She said things like, 'I hope those animal-rights people don't wreck

153

the place. Hundreds are threatening to demonstrate. We've had one murder at Ancombe. I hope we don't have another.' When she got tired, Roy took over.

Then Agatha phoned Guy. 'I saw it on the news,' he said. 'Let's just hope we get something out of it. It isn't your fault, Agatha.'

As if to complete the disaster, when Agatha and Roy awoke the next morning, a steady drenching rain was falling from lowering skies.

Roy tried to console her. 'You made arrangements for rain, Aggie. Remember? All the events can take place in the marquees.'

'But we were to march to the spring behind the village band,' mourned Agatha, 'and I pictured it all sunny. Now all we'll get's a straggling row of umbrella-covered people.'

'We can only do our best,' sighed Roy.

Agatha expected the Freemont brothers to blame her for the weather, but they both seemed quite calm and cheerful. 'Everything looks quite jolly,' said Guy, 'and loads of people are beginning to arrive.'

'What about the press?'

'They're already getting liquored up in the press tent.'

'I'd better go and join them. Come along, Roy.'

Entering the press tent, Agatha's expert eye ranged over the assembled journalists and her heart sank. There was the *Birmingham Mercury* – good paper, that – the *Cotswold Journal*, the *Gloucester Echo*, Midlands Television and so on, all local. Where were the nationals?

She moved among them, chatting brightly away. Lord Pendlebury would open the fête at eleven in the main tent, then everyone would have a chance to buy things at the stalls. At twelve the village band would lead a procession to the spring.

When Agatha went to the main tent to hear Lord Pendlebury's speech, she knew the whole thing was a ghastly failure. The rain dampened everything, despite the flowers and heaters inside the tents. The ground was muddy and spongy underfoot and the day was cold. A malicious wind had got up and flapped the sodden canvas.

Lord Pendlebury made a long and boring speech about his military service during World War II. He did not mention the water company and Agatha was suddenly convinced he had totally forgotten why he was there. A baby began to cry. One little boy kicked his sister in the shins; she began to scream and other children screamed in competition.

Teenagers who had travelled down from Birmingham in the hope of seeing The Pretty

Girls were drinking beer from cans and looking surly.

When the time for the procession to the spring arrived, all Agatha wanted to do was run away and hide. The plan was that she and the Freemont brothers and Lord Pendlebury would lead the procession. Originally it was to be led by The Pretty Girls. And how often Agatha had fondly imagined that original picture. The crowds, the laughter, the jolly band, the sun beating down.

She saw James talking to an attractive woman in the refreshment tent. He was laughing at something she was saying. Agatha's misery was complete.

She found Guy at her elbow. 'Where were you during Lord Pendlebury's speech?' she asked.

'Off somewhere thinking about getting drunk but not doing it. Let's go and join the procession.'

'How are the band to play in this rain?'

'The band leader assures me they're used to it. Get the press and tell them we're off.'

The press had obviously been making up for lack of a newsworthy event by swapping stories and drinking hard. They looked reluctant to leave, but they dutifully picked up their gear and followed Agatha out into the rain.

As they approached the spring, the band had opted to play 'Bridge Over Troubled

Water'. It sounds like a dirge, thought Agatha, feeling she would like to cry, and this is like a funeral procession.

'Oh, my God,' said Guy, grabbing Agatha's arm.

'What?'

'Look there!'

The music behind them faltered off into silence except for the drummer, who did not have a clear view of what was transfixing the rest of them.

Robina Toynbee hung head down over her garden wall. Blood from a gaping wound in her head dripped down into the spring. Boom, boom, boom, went the drum. Then it too was silent.

A woman screamed, high and long and loud.

Chaos erupted.

The galvanized press pushed and shoved to get photographs.

Guy whipped out his mobile phone and thrust it at Agatha.

'Find a quiet corner and get on to the nationals – quick!'

'But the police –'

'I'll get them. Go!' He gave her a little shove.

Agatha thrust her way round the edge of the crowd and then ran to the deserted press tent. She sat down and poured herself a stiff brandy and then started to phone while inside her grew a loathing for her job.

She was joined by Roy. She pushed him a list of the media she had already phoned. 'I'll do some,' said Roy. 'God, I feel sick. That poor woman.'

'She called me last night, and the news about The Pretty Girls put it straight out of my head,' said Agatha.

'Never mind, let's get on with this. Peter Freemont wants you to mug up some sort of speech for him to make to the press.'

Agatha opened up her briefcase and took out her laptop and switched it on. Almost without thought, the words came. 'Ancombe Water, the Water of Life, will be successful because it is the best mineral water on the market. The unfortunate murders will not stop the company from producing it or believing in their fine product. There have already been suggestions that some unscrupulous rival company is going to any lengths to sabotage the launch,' and so on.

Dimly she was aware of Roy's voice chattering away.

Among the bottles of booze in front of her, Ancombe Water glittered whitely, the skull on the label etched in black, a little row of serried skulls grinning at her.

'I'll need to go home and run this off on the printer,' she said.

'I brought it,' said Roy, who had just rung off after another call. 'I mean, I've got mine. It's stashed in my case over in the corner. I'll get it.'

'When can we expect the nationals?'

'The stringers will be here any minute and then the heavy mob should make it, traffic willing, in about an hour and a half. We're going to be busy. Hold on a minute, Aggie. Let's have a drink and sit quietly. I don't know about you, but right now I hate this effing job and I want to go and join the Peace Corps.'

'You know, you're quite a decent fellow, Roy. I was thinking pretty much the same thing.'

'Marry me?'

Agatha laughed. 'You don't really mean that. I've already had brandy. I'd better stick to that. It's going to be a long day.'

Roy poured two brandies. 'Listen to that rain. Getting worse. Oh, my gawd, we told the nationals that there would be dark doings. The police are going to think we, or the Freemonts, bumped off that poor woman for publicity.'

'Bit far-fetched. But I tell you one thing for sure, Roy. I've gone off Guy Freemont. Oh, I know he's got a business to save, but he could at least have got the police and an ambulance instead of handing me his mobile and telling me to get the nationals.'

'Were you sweet on him?'

'A bit. Maybe – no. I was flattered, him being so much younger and so good-looking and what with James snubbing me at every turn and then going off and investigating on his own. None of it seems important now. I didn't like Robina, but who would do this to her, and why? She had been getting those threatening letters and yet she wouldn't show them to the police.'

'Talking about the police, you'd better run off your deathless prose. They'll be with us soon. Did you see any of your suspects around? I mean, it must have happened just before the procession set off.'

'No. I wasn't really looking for them. Just glad that none of them had come up to insult me.'

Roy plugged his printer into Agatha's computer.

As the speech began to churn out, the press tent began to fill up. Voices were soon heard on mobiles, laptops placed among the bottles and glasses.

'Water of Life,' Agatha heard one reporter shout down the phone. 'Water of Death would be a good headline.'

Portia appeared beside Agatha. Her tweed suit, thought Agatha sourly, looked as if it had been painted on. How she managed to get it so tight and yet so smooth must be some miracle of tailoring. 'Have you got Mr Peter's speech?' she asked.

Agatha gathered up the pages from the printer tray and handed them to her. 'I suggest that Guy makes this speech.'

'Why?'

'He's better-looking. Look good on television.'

Portia leaned forward and whispered, 'Don't you find your infatuation with Guy a little sad at your age?'

'Piss off,' said Agatha furiously.

'What was that about?' asked Roy.

'Never mind. Have we phoned everyone?'

'Yes, and with this lot telling their news desks, and their news desks telling London, I should think everyone knows. It'll be out on the radio news anyway.'

The rest of the day passed in a blur of hectic activity for Agatha. Peter Freemont made the speech she had written. There were cameras everywhere, flashing and clicking. Television reporters did their job, which had everyone they could think of making a statement, preceded by the eternal TV film cliché of having the interviewee walking. Why, Agatha wondered, did people have to be seen walking before they faced the cameras?

Boom microphones, oblong and furry, were held above heads. The rain drummed relentlessly down. Children, thwarted of their performance in the talent competition, screamed and cried if they were very young and moodily sulked and dug up chunks of grass with their Doc Martens if they were older.

To Agatha's horror, she came across Lord Pendlebury making a statement to the press. 'It's all the fault of incomers,' he said. 'Nasty people. Never had this trouble when people who belonged in the cities stayed in the cities.'

She quickly moved in front of him and said loudly, 'We owe much to Lord Pendlebury for lending his support to the launch of Ancombe Water. He will agree with me that anything that brings business and jobs to a rural area is welcome. Do you know that the Ancombe Water Company gave first priority in jobs to the villagers of Ancombe?'

And so on, until the disgruntled lord shuffled off and the press yawned.

Finally she and Roy had to sit down in a police trailer facing Bill Wong.

'Now, you two,' he said severely, 'what on earth were you about, hinting to the press that something awful was going to happen? I can tell you that there are mutterings amongst them that Robina Toynbee was murdered because of a publicity stunt.'

'That's ridiculous,' said Agatha.

'So why did you say such a thing?'

Agatha looked miserable. 'I felt the press were beginning to lose interest. I didn't hint

162

at murder. I hinted there might be another demonstration. It could have well happened. It's my job, Bill. Had to get them here.'

'You've got the lot now,' said Bill grimly.

'Why wasn't Robina at the festivities anyway?' asked Roy.

'Part of the arrangement was that Robina Toynbee was to be at her garden wall over the spring when the procession arrived. So she told her neighbour.'

'And who made this arrangement?' asked Agatha. 'I heard nothing about it. The Freemonts?'

'No, luckily for them, or I really would have begun to think it was some macabre publicity stunt. According to this neighbour, a Mrs Brown, Robina thought up the whole thing herself. She was miffed because she had not been asked to make a speech, considering it was her water. So she planned to be at her garden wall and, when the procession arrived, make a speech. It was found on the grass beside her – her notes, I mean.'

'Oh, help!' Agatha stared at Bill, wide-eyed. 'Robina left a message for me last night. She wanted me to phone her. Then I got the news about the pop group not being able to make it and I forgot all about her. Maybe she just wanted to tell me about her speech.'

'Could be,' said Bill. 'Did you save the message?'

'Yes, it'll still be there.'

'I'll get along to your place later and listen to it.'

'So it looks as if we're back to the ones on the parish council who didn't want the water company to go ahead,' said Agatha. 'The againsts are Bill Allen, Andy Stiggs and Mary Owen. Where were they?'

'Mary Owen was at home. She said she didn't want to have anything to do with it. Bill Allen says he was at his garden centre, but as his staff of two young people had been given an hour off to go to the fête, we have no witnesses. Andy Stiggs says he was working in his garden.'

'In this weather?'

'He says the heavy rain had battered a climbing rose and he was tying it up. With all that shrubbery in Robina Toynbee's garden, anyone could have hidden there and as soon as she got to the garden wall, struck her a blow from behind. Most villagers were already at the fête.'

'Yes, and when we walked along to the spring, apart from those from the fête who were accompanying the procession,' said Agatha, 'there was no one about.'

'I am going to take statements from both of you,' said Bill. 'I want you to go over carefully and clearly why you hinted to the press that there might be trouble and then what you were both doing at the time of the murder.'

It seemed to take a long time.

'I need a drink,' said Agatha when they were finally free. 'Let's go and see the Freemonts. I really want to get away from here.'

They found Guy, Peter and Portia in the press tent. Portia was laughing at something Guy was saying, her hand on his arm. Agatha's eyes narrowed. Then she reminded herself that she did not want to have anything more to do with Guy, romantically, that is. She had a craving to be her age, act her age, and stop worrying about wrinkles and sagging flesh.

'Agatha!' cried Guy, detaching himself from Portia. He gathered her in his arms and gave her a kiss. 'Isn't it all too awful? But you handled things magnificently.'

'I don't know,' said Agatha, awkwardly disengaging herself. 'I heard one reporter suggesting a good headline would be the Water of Death.'

'Don't worry. You should know. By the time all this blows over, all they'll remember is the name. We'll be world headlines tomorrow. We've got a great marketing manager. We've sent complimentary supplies to every restaurant round about, and to the top restaurants in London. It's a clever bottle. It would have been cheaper to put the water in plastic ones, but we think the success of Perrier, say, is that because it's in a glass bottle with a screw-top, it doesn't go flat, like the stuff in the plastic ones.'

'Have you made statements to the police?'

'Yes, everything's over and done with. Don't worry, Agatha. It's all worked out all right.'

'Well, the arrangement was that my job would finish on the day of the fête,' said Agatha. 'I won't be seeing much of either of you again.'

'Did we make that arrangement?'

'Yes,' said Roy, moving forward. 'I've got the week off, Aggie. So if you can put up with me putting up with you, I'd like to stay on.'

'Okay,' said Agatha.

'Wait a minute,' said Peter quickly. 'Perhaps you could drop into the office on Monday. We haven't got a replacement for you. We needed an expert to get this off the ground, but now with the murder and all, we could do with your services.'

'Let me have a week off,' said Agatha quickly, 'and I'll think about it.'

She and Roy left the press tent and emerged into blazing sunlight. 'Typical,' said Agatha, and then she began to cry.

Chapter Seven

Bill Wong arrived at Agatha's cottage with Chief Inspector Wilkes and a policewoman. They listened carefully to Agatha's answering service.

'She sounds agitated,' said Wilkes.

'Robina could have received more of these threatening letters,' said Agatha. 'She'd been getting them and I told her to take them to the police, but she wouldn't. I told you about them, didn't I, Bill?'

'You'd better go over again, for the chief inspector's benefit, everything you've found out.'

So Agatha began at the beginning. It all seemed such a muddle, and the idea that one of the respectable members of the Ancombe Parish Council should suddenly turn murderer was too strange to believe.

There was a ring at the doorbell.

Roy went to answer it and came back followed by James.

Agatha looked at him stonily, in her heart blaming him for her affair with Guy.

'Good,' said Bill, looking up from his notes. 'We were going to call on you, and this saves time. Do you think any of those Save Our Foxes people could be mad enough to commit murder?'

'Could be,' said James, sinking down in an armchair. 'It might explain the second murder, but surely not the first. No one knew which way old Struthers meant to vote.'

'It's a pity about Mary Owen,' said Agatha. 'She was my prime suspect. She's strong enough and nasty enough.'

'There seems enough proof that she was where she said she was, at her sister's.'

'Have you thought about the water company?' asked James. 'They've got world-wide publicity out of today. They would have got very little if it hadn't been for the murder. No pop group. Nothing to draw them.'

'I think that's ridiculous,' said Agatha hotly.

'Well, you would.' James's voice was cold. 'But if we can keep emotional involvement out of this and look at it objectively, this publicity is worth millions to the Freemont brothers.'

'If you keep jealousy out of it,' said Roy, 'and think about it, it shouldn't do them all that much good. Two dead people dripping blood into that spring!'

'Why on earth should I be jealous?'

168

'Because of Aggie's ring-a-ding wish Guy Freemont.'

'Rubbish,' said James.

'There is nothing between me and Guy Freemont,' howled Agatha.

'Oh, so his car just happens to be parked outside your cottage all night by accident,' said James nastily. 'What were you doing all night? Drinking water?'

'Get out of here!' shouted Agatha, tears starting to her eyes.

'Calm down, all of you,' said Wilkes. 'I want the three of you to report to police headquarters tomorrow morning and we'll go over it again.'

James left with the police.

'What now?' asked Roy. 'Should we think of somewhere for dinner?'

'Let's go for a drive first,' said Agatha. 'I know, we'll go into Mircester. There's a new Chinese restaurant.'

'Just look at the weather,' said Roy bitterly as a flaming sunset settled over the Cotswold Hills and the first stars glimmered faintly in a perfect sky.

'There's a curse on the whole venture,' said Agatha gloomily. 'Perhaps, after dinner, we should go for a long walk and tire ourselves out.'

'I'm tired already.' Roy yawned.

'I mean I want to be exhausted when I go to bed or I'll keep seeing dead Robina.'

They parked in the square at Mircester and walked to the Chinese restaurant. Agatha grabbed Roy's arm before he could go in and hissed, 'Look who's sitting at the window.'

Roy looked and saw a middle-aged Chinese man with a droopy moustache and what appeared to be a typical Gloucestershire housewife.

'So?'

'That's Bill Wong's parents.'

'The father's Chinese, surely. Good sign.'

'No, it's not. They like terrible food.'

'Oh, well, where to? I'm not really hungry.'

'Me neither. Let's walk for a bit.'

They set off in a westward direction, glancing aimlessly in shops, both wrapped in their own thoughts.

Finally they reached the suburbs and walked along a quiet street lined with villas.

'Am I seeing things?' asked Agatha, breaking the silence. 'Or is that Mary Owen just turning in at that gate?'

Under the light of a street lamp a little way ahead, the tall figure certainly looked like Mary Owen.

Agatha quickened her pace. 'Mary!' she called.

The woman stopped, her hand resting on the gate, and looked back at them.

'Mary!' said Agatha again.

'I am Mary's sister,' said the woman. 'I am Mrs Darcy, and who are you?'

'I am Agatha Raisin, and this is Roy Silver.'

'I have heard of you. You're that interfering busybody who fancies herself a detective. Good evening.' Mrs Darcy went in and shut the gate with a clang. Agatha and Roy walked on.

'Did you notice the remarkable resemblance?' said Agatha excitedly. 'They could be twins. Why didn't Bill say something about it?'

'So what?'

'That's how the alibi could have been established. The neighbours could have thought they were seeing Mary when in fact they were seeing Mrs Darcy.'

'Wait a bit. The curtains were drawn back on the evening of the murder. They were seen dining together.'

'But dinner doesn't take all evening.' Agatha gave a skip of excitement.

'When was it you went to the spring?'

'It was nearly midnight. They're vague about the time of death, but put it somewhere earlier in the evening. Now, when you and I think about dinnertime, we think about eight o'clock or after, but a lot of people have it much earlier.'

'We could ask the neighbours.'

'I've a feeling if we did that, Mary and her sister would report us for intrusion of privacy.

171

We'll ask Bill tomorrow. Roy, I'd begun not to care who committed the first murder. But two! And James going ahead and investigating without me! By God, I'd like to find out who did it just to see his face.'

'I'm really tired now,' complained Roy, 'and hungry. Look at the time, Agatha.' He thrust his Rolex watch in front of Agatha's eyes. 'Eleven o'clock. A lot of the pubs are shut. We'll be lucky to find anywhere open.'

They trudged the long way back into the centre of Mircester. 'The Chinese is still open.'

'Oh, let's just have a bowl of something, then,' said Agatha.

The restaurant was nearly empty. 'Let's just order one of the set meals,' said Agatha. 'I'm too weary to wade through the menu.'

The food was delicious. 'So we wandered around for nothing,' said Roy.

'Not nothing. We know now that Mary looks remarkably like her sister.'

'Can I have something to drink? You're driving.'

'I thought you'd gone off alcohol.'

'It's the stress.'

'You know what they say – once you start saying you need a drink, you're in trouble.'

'But that's your favourite line, Aggie dear.'

'Well, these are exceptional circumstances.' Agatha called the waiter over and asked for the wine list. 'We'll get a cab home. James can drive us in the morning.'

'Oho! I thought you wanted nothing to do with him.'

'We're in competition now and I want to know what he's up to.'

Agatha slept heavily and awoke to find it was nine in the morning. She let out a squawk of alarm and phoned James.

'Yes, what is it, Agatha?' Crisp, very crisp.

'I've left my car in Mircester and wondered if you could give me and Roy a lift over to Mircester this morning.'

There was a short silence and then James said curtly, 'I'll pick you up at ten.'

Agatha shot upstairs, calling on Roy to wake up as she did so. She washed and made herself up with care.

Roy and Agatha walked along to James's cottage promptly at ten. He got in beside the wheel of his car. Roy made as if to get into the front passenger seat, but Agatha jerked him back.

'Only trying to save you embarrassment, Aggie,' muttered Roy, getting into the back seat.

'So who do you think is committing these murders?' asked James.

'I favour Mary Owen.'

'Why?'

'Just a hunch.'

'It's more than that,' said Roy eagerly. 'We took a walk in Mircester last night and we came across that sister, Mrs Darcy. She's the spitting image of Mary.'

I'll kill you, Roy, thought Agatha, who had been hoping to keep back that bit of information.

'But Bill said something about the neighbours having seen them having dinner together.'

'But Aggie didn't find Struthers's body until near midnight. Mary could have driven over from Mircester, bumped him off somewhere and dumped the body at the spring. Or she could have been helped by her sister.'

'I don't like that idea,' said James. 'I would like to know more about the Freemonts.'

'You can't think it's them,' said Agatha.

'Why not? They may have known Struthers was going to vote against the water.'

'But what about Robina?' asked Agatha.

'Well, she could have changed her mind.'

'Too late to do that,' Roy pointed out. 'She must have signed something and that speech of hers – or rather the notes for it – if there had been anything about stopping the water company, it would have been in those notes and the police would have said something.'

'True.' James negotiated a bend too quickly and Agatha was thrown against him. She struggled upright. That touch of her shoulder against James's had sent an electrical charge through her body. 'What is the background of the Freemonts, Agatha?'

'Business in Hong Kong. Rag trade. Moved over here.'

'I know all that. Anything else? Either of them married or been married?'

'Guy isn't married,' said Agatha quickly. 'I don't know about Peter.'

'How do you know Guy isn't married?'

'I just know,' said Agatha crossly. 'Oh, look out!'

James braked suddenly. A small deer darted in front of the car and vanished into the dappled shade of a wood at the side of the road.

James drove on more slowly. 'I mean,' Agatha continued, 'he hasn't tried to hide me off in obscure restaurants.'

'His wife need not be living in the area,' said James.

'I still think the murderer is one of the parish council,' said Roy 'They all seem pretty nasty.'

'If there is one thing I hate,' said Agatha, 'it's environmental groups, them with their open-toed sandals and open-toed minds.'

'They can be a pain.' James accelerated along the Fosse. 'But someone's got to put the brakes on some of the time. Do you know what they did with some of those lovely old Georgian houses in Mayfair? They're supposed to preserve the façade, so they take down the building behind in such a way that the whole thing collapses. Oops! Sorry, they say, and build some horrible modern box instead. Then take Greenpeace.'

'Please,' muttered Roy sotto-voce from the back seat.

'They often come across as a bunch of publicity seekers who never actually do anything constructive, and yet it was their complaints about the filth of British beaches that started the clean-up.'

'Interesting discussion.' Agatha sighed. 'It's not getting us any nearer finding out who murdered Robina or Struthers.'

'Could you not,' said James, 'get them all together in one room? I mean, Agatha, as a rep of the water company, you could send out invitations to a get-together. A sort of bury-the-hatchet meeting? Offer them champagne and a buffet. Something that'll draw them.'

'It might work.' Agatha thought quickly. 'They'll all feel under suspicion and that might draw them together. I'll think about it. I know, my garden's looking pretty nice. I could hold a garden party.'

'I'll pay half,' said James. 'I shouldn't think the water company would stump up.'

'They might.' Agatha sounded cautious. 'I mean, they still want me to work for them, so

I might put it to them that it would be a good-will gesture. In fact, after we're finished at the police station, we could drive over to the company and I'll suggest it.'

So much for competing with James, thought Roy. But he knew if Agatha worked a little longer for the company, then his firm would get a substantial cut and he would be the golden boy.

To Agatha it seemed strange that she and James, who had only recently been at logger-heads, should be conversing so amiably. But then James had always been like that.

As she made her statement at the police station, she could not help remembering the other times she had made statements to the police along with James. Did he think of that? Did he think ever of the times they had made love?

It was always hard to tell with James.

After they had made their statements, they drove out to the water company. It was a hive of activity, not the semi-deserted place it had been when Agatha had first arrived.

While James parked, Agatha whipped out her powder compact and peered anxiously at her face in the little mirror, all her fear of wrinkles returning now that she was to see Guy.

In reception they waited until Portia came to fetch them. She smiled at James and Roy but not at Agatha. She was wearing a tailored jacket over tailored shorts which exposed her long, long legs in sheer black tights.

She led them into the boardroom. Guy and Peter were waiting for them.

'What's this delegation?' asked Guy.

Agatha explained that they had all gone together to police headquarters to make statements and since Roy was her house guest and from head office, and James Lacey, her neighbour, had kindly driven them, she had just brought them along.

'So are you going to work for us for a bit longer?' asked Peter.

'That's what I want to discuss with you. These murders have caused a lot of bad feeling in Ancombe. I thought it might be good public relations to throw a garden party for the members of Ancombe Parish Council.'

Guy looked amused. 'I can't see the press turning up for anything like that.'

'It's more of a goodwill mission than a press party,' said Agatha.

'I appreciate your motives,' said Peter, 'but we've already done enough for that village and we have to work to our budget. I cannot see the point of funding anything that doesn't get us in the newspapers.'

'Then I'll do it myself,' said Agatha. With James beside her, she wanted more than ever to distance herself from Guy. 'And as a matter of fact, I'm going to stop representing you. The launch is over. The water's on the market. There is really no need any longer to engage me.'

Portia, who had been sitting at the end of the table, said suddenly, 'I've been telling you and telling you, I am perfectly capable of doing the public relations job. The launch was a fiasco.'

'I didn't plan the rain, the murder or The Pretty Girls scandal,' said Agatha.

'I said, didn't I, Guy, that The Pretty Girls were a bad idea?' said Portia. 'I mean, one heard *murmurs*.'

'Murmurs that you didn't bother telling me about.' Agatha glared.

Portia shrugged her elegant shoulders.

'We don't want to lose you,' said Guy.

'That's very flattering.' Agatha got to her feet. 'But I'm going to be too busy. Give the job to Miss Sunshine over there.'

Guy rushed to hold the door open for her. 'Dinner tonight?' he asked.

'Can't,' said Agatha. 'Got Roy staying. I'll phone you.'

Portia led them out to reception. Agatha nodded to her curtly and walked away. To her horror, she heard James ask Portia, 'Are you free for dinner one evening?'

Agatha stopped in her tracks, her shoulders rigid.

She heard Portia laugh and say, 'I don't think my boyfriend would approve, but why

179

don't you give me your phone number anyway?'

Agatha, with Roy behind her, walked out to James's car and stood fuming.

'He's sure one of the Freemonts did it,' said Roy in a soothing voice. 'That's why he asked her out.'

But Agatha's mind was full of pictures of James dining by candle-light with the beautiful Portia, James taking Portia home, James staying the night.

'So do we still go ahead with the garden party?' asked James when he joined them.

'May as well. I'll try to get them here for next Sunday. Will you stay on for that, Roy?'

'Think, if you don't mind, I'd better get back to London tonight,' said Roy. He was considering that it was one thing to stay on with Agatha Raisin, prize PR for the water company, but quite another, in his boss's eyes, to stay on with plain unemployed Mrs Raisin.

Agatha flashed him a cynical look. Roy's job would always come first.

James dropped them at Agatha's car and they followed him home.

When they arrived back in Carsely, James said, 'When are we going to discuss the arrangements for this garden party, Agatha?'

Roy had got out of the car first and was waiting on Agatha's doorstep.

James and Agatha were standing outside their cars on the pavement.

'If you want to work with me,' said Agatha in a low voice.

'Truce,' said James. 'Let's just forget all the hard things we've been saying to each other. We've worked well together in the past.'

'Okay,' said Agatha, half-torn between elation and dread, dread that she was being sucked back down into all the miseries caused by proximity to James. 'So maybe we should get on the phone and invite them all?'

'All right. We'll use my phone.'

'Right, I'll tell Roy to pack. I'll see you in a few minutes.'

'I'm going to James's to make some phone calls,' said Agatha. 'I'll leave you to pack.'

To her surprise, there was no argument from Roy about being left out. But Roy was glad of an opportunity to phone his boss on his own without Agatha listening. If there was any credit to be got out of the launch, he would take it; if there was any blame, then Agatha could shoulder it.

Agatha walked along to James's cottage. The door was standing open and she walked into the book-lined living-room. 'Sit down and I'll bring the coffee,' shouted James from the kitchen.

Agatha took out her compact and dusted her nose with powder.

She stuffed it back in her handbag as James came in carrying a tray with two mugs.

'Now,' said James, 'let's see who we've got. Against the water company we have Mary Owen, Bill Allen and Andy Stiggs. For, we have Jane Cutler, Angela Buckley and Fred Shaw.' He produced a notebook. 'I've got their names and phone numbers here. Drink your coffee and we'll start phoning. Who's going to do the phoning?'

'I think you'd better,' said Agatha. 'I seem to bring out the beast in them.'

'And what're we having? And how do we know the weather will be fine for a garden party?'

'I'll tell you why the weather'll be fine,' said Agatha bitterly. 'Because it's done its worst to drown out the launch and the long-range forecast is good. Do you think they will come? Mary Owen's bound to refuse. I keep wondering who could have murdered Robina. Was it all really because of the water? I wonder who gets her cottage and her money?'

'I heard someone say she had a son. Anyway, here goes. I'll start with the worst. Mary Owen.'

'Good luck. But I don't think you'll get very far. Do you know her?'

'Yes, as a matter of fact, I called on her before I went off to join Save Our Foxes. We got on all right.'

182

'You might have told me!'

'We're having a truce – remember?'

'Oh, all right, but I want a cigarette. I'll take it out into the garden. Are we just going to have the people from the parish council? It might be viewed as a bit of a snub by our friends in the village if they're not invited.'

'Don't let them know you've resigned from the water company, then. Let them think it's business.'

Agatha went out into James's small front garden, sat down on the doorstep and lit a cigarette.

She listened to him talking on the phone. That easy laugh of his! There was a lot of the actor in James. When he had finished phoning, should she confront him, say something like 'Where do we stand now, James?'

But he might answer something to the effect that they stood nowhere, nowhere at all.

'Mary,' she heard him say in a cajoling voice, 'it's just a get-together, champagne and eats, all paid for by the water company. Look at it this way: you've all got to put this behind you and work together for the better good of the parish. Yes, a good opportunity to mend fences. What time? Oh, twelve or twelve-thirty. Good, see you then.'

So Mary was coming.

Agatha finished her cigarette and threw the stub over the hedge and out into the road, where it landed at the feet of Mrs Darry, who picked up the stub and threw it back. 'Don't you have an ashtray?' she demanded angrily. 'We're not in London now.'

'If you're so concerned about a clean environment, then stop that nasty little dog of yours pissing and defecating outside my home,' yelled Agatha.

'And show a bit of decorum,' shouted Mrs Darry, her face puce. 'You're showing your knickers.'

Agatha angrily pulled her skirt down, which had ridden up about her knees.

If only it could turn out to be Mrs Darry. If only something could happen to remove her from Carsely.

She moodily lit another cigarette. Some doctors in Britain were refusing to treat smokers for illness. Why? With all the taxes on tobacco that the smoker paid, they should be getting first-class free treatment. Why smokers? Why not drunks? Why not fat people? Bloody nanny state. Mrs Darry had put Agatha into a foul temper. People flapped their hands in your face and said, 'I don't want to die from passive smoking,' and then they got in their cars and drove off, blasting carcinogens into the night air. The cigarette tasted foul. Come to think of it, all cigarettes tasted foul after the first three of the day. But come to think of it, too, just when one thought of giving up, some puritan would pop up to lecture sanctimoniously on the evils of nicotine and drive the will to stop farther away. The only time the cigarettes tasted just fine all day long was during the annual No Smoking Day. Funny that, mused Agatha. If they changed it to Smoke-Till-You-Drop Day, probably a lot more addicts would give up.

'You can come in now,' called James. 'That's the lot. They're all coming.'

Agatha rose and went back in.

'What about food?' he asked.

'Normally I'd get people like Mrs Bloxby to help me,' said Agatha, 'but as we are supposed to be running this on behalf of the water company, we'd better hire a catering firm. We'll have something like cold salmon and salad and strawberries and cream.'

'The strawberries are past their best.'

'People eat strawberries, no matter what. They like the idea. It's like fish and chips. What a good idea, particularly on a cold night, you think, all warm and hot and golden and smelling divine. In fact, all you get is a sodden packet of greasy food which lies like lead in your stomach.'

'What about tables and things?'

'There's only six of them and two of us – that's eight. My kitchen table's quite large and I'll borrow a table from the school hall for the champagne. They can't all be hard drinkers. A bottle a head is generous enough.'

'Right. What I suggest is that you pay for the lot and let me know how much it comes to and I'll pay half.'

'I feel I might be able to get the water company to actually foot the bill. I didn't press hard enough.'

'Ah, but that would mean the Freemonts might attend as well, and the purpose of this party is to see how they act once they're all together.'

'I thought you suspected the Freemonts.'

'I'll get around to them.'

Agatha looked at him thoughtfully. 'So we're back in business again, James.'

'Mmm?' He looked up from some notes he had been making. 'Oh, yes, back in business.'

'Don't you feel any awkwardness?'

'Don't let's get into that, Agatha.'

No, thought Agatha, don't let's ever talk about feelings, about the times we made love, about the rows, about pain. Let's just go on like a couple of bachelors interested in crime.

'I'd better go and talk to Roy.'

'You do that,' he said cheerfully.

Why did I say anything? mourned Agatha as she let herself into her cottage. I promised myself I wouldn't. What else did I expect? A human response? From *James*? Rats!

Roy came clattering down the stairs. 'How did you get on with lover boy?'

'If you mean James, cut it out. They're all coming.'

'What about little me?'

Agatha suddenly didn't want Roy around. She was already planning what to wear.

'Skip it this time, Roy,' she said. 'I'll be too busy to cope with a house guest.'

Roy looked hurt. 'Be like that. But remember, I won't always be at your beck and call when you need me.'

'I thought your only interest in me was to further your career.'

'I think I'll get an earlier train if there is one.' Roy looked offended.

'We'll have lunch. You can get the afternoon one.'

It was a silent lunch.

'Look,' said Agatha, relenting over the coffee. 'I haven't been straight with you. I really do want James all to myself.'

'Waste of space, sweetie.'

'Perhaps.' Agatha sighed. 'Let's not quarrel. I'll drive you to Oxford. We'll have a better choice of trains.'

'You can do something to make up.'

'What?'

'I've always wanted to punt.'

'What? At Oxford? On the river?'

'Yes.'

'All right. Finish your coffee and we'll go now.'

Agatha managed to find a parking place in the High and they walked down to Magdalen Bridge and down the steps at the side to the landing-stage.

'I haven't been here before,' said Agatha. 'I didn't know the river would be so narrow here. And there are so many punts out. Are you sure you want to try this?'

'Yes, yes.' Roy gave an excited little skip. 'I read about it in a Sunday supplement.'

When they asked for a punt, the boatman told them the charge was eight pounds for an hour, twenty-five pounds deposit and to leave identification.

'I'm a bit short,' said Roy. 'Could you . . .?'

'Oh, all right.' Agatha paid the money and left her driving licence.

'I feel this is a mistake.' Agatha scrambled on to the seat of the punt. Roy seized the long pole. 'There are paddles,' said Agatha. 'Wouldn't it be a good idea to paddle to a quiet bit?' There were not only punts but rowing boats.

The boatman pushed them out. Roy dug the pole in and pushed. The punt swung in a wide circle and bumped into a puntload of students.

'Steady on,' called one.

Roy was pink with embarrassment. 'I'll use the paddle.' He shipped the pole and crouched down in the bow and paddled. After a few false starts and a few more bumps, they headed up the river.

Then he stood up and took up the pole again. Agatha lay back in the punt and decided to ignore Roy's amateurish efforts. The sun was filtering down through the trees. Conservatories were glittering on one side, a cricket pavilion on the other, willow trees trailing in the water, dappled light and peace. But not a typically English scene, thought Agatha, looking at the students. I always imagined everyone in white and ladies with parasols. The students all looked terribly young and undernourished and seemed to favour black shirts, tatty jeans and pony-tails – the men, that is. They came from a mixture of nationalities. She was roused from her reverie as a branch banged against her head.

'Look where you're going!'

'Sorry, just getting the hang of this.'

James. Would she and James ever get together again? Would she ever stop thinking about him? Why was it Guy meant so little? Perhaps because sex did not mean intimacy. Talk was intimacy. Friendship was intimacy. Perhaps if she had practised friendship a bit more in earlier life, she would know better how to handle him. Or just leave him alone,

said a cynical voice in her brain. It's sick. You
need an exorcist.

'I'm really getting good at this.'

'Can't you steer a straight course?' asked
Agatha. 'You nearly banged into that rowing-
boat.'

'We're doing fine,' said Roy 'You just dig the
pole in, Aggie, and thrust –'

To Agatha's horror, he *pole-vaulted* and
landed face-down on the grassy bank while
Agatha and the punt went shooting off in the
other direction. The punt hit the opposite bank
with force as she instinctively rose to her feet,
and Agatha was catapulted into the river.

Roy jumped in to save her, swam towards
her and made ineffectual grabs at her hair.

'Leave me alone!' shouted Agatha. 'My
handbag's in the punt. Get it. I mean, get
the punt.'

Under the delighted gaze of a boatload of
Japanese, Roy seized the rope at the front of
the punt and towed it to the bank on which he
had first landed. Agatha swam after him.

He helped her out.

'All right?' called a Japanese student. 'Very
funny. You in a film?'

'No,' said Agatha curtly. She rounded on
Roy. 'Let's just get back in that damned instru-
ment of torture and get back.'

As the amused Japanese looked on, they

got back on board. 'We'll pull you back,' shouted one.

'No, we'll manage,' said Roy.

'No, we won't. That would be great,' said Agatha.

They sat in the punt dripping wet, faces red with mortification as the Japanese towed them back to the landing-stage. A group of English students were waiting to greet these Japanese friends and they laughed and clapped as Roy and Agatha, bedraggled and miserable, were helped from the punt.

They walked together up the High, a yard apart, and people turned to stare at them.

'I am taking you straight to the station,' said Agatha when they got in the car. 'You've got your luggage. You can change in the station loo.'

'I'm really, really sorry,' said Roy meekly. 'It was something I'd always wanted to do.'

Agatha drove in grim silence.

'Look, Aggie. I left school at fifteen, never went to university. We all have dreams. Punting at Oxford was one of mine.'

Agatha slowed down.

'I tell you what we'll do,' she said. 'Dry yourself and change at the station. Then take a cab up to Marks and Spencer and buy me some dry clothes and then I'll change. I'll take you for tea at the Randolph.'

* * *

Three hours later, Agatha made her way back to Carsely wearing a new outfit of blouse and skirt, along with the new underwear underneath and a pair of new flat shoes which were extremely comfortable. Roy had enjoyed his tea and they had begun to laugh helplessly over their exploits on the river. Agatha smiled reminiscently. She could not remember laughing so hard in such a long time.

As she drove down the winding country lane which led to the village of Carsely under the arching tunnel of green, green trees, she felt like some sort of animal heading homeward to a comfortable burrow.

And since her fall in the river, she hadn't thought of James, not once.

That evening she went to a meeting of the Carsely Ladies' Society at the vicarage. Mrs Bloxby served tea and sandwiches in the vicarage garden. Mrs Darry was not present and Agatha entertained the rest of them with a highly embroidered tale of her punting adventure.

The meeting then got down to business. The society had decided to put on a concert. Agatha groaned. The concerts were a nightmare of boredom. Not one of them had a bit of talent and yet so many were delighted to get up on the stage and sing in cracked voices.

And yet they attended other concerts in other villages and the performances were just as awful. Mrs Bloxby had explained to her gently that everyone secretly wanted to perform on the stage and this was a chance for them all to get their moment in the sun. Agatha noticed, however, that the vicar's wife, like herself, never performed.

Conversation after the official meeting turned to the murders in Ancombe. 'I've got all the members of the parish council coming to a garden party at my place,' said Agatha. 'I haven't invited any of you because the water company is paying for it and it's public relations business.'

'They're a funny lot,' said Miss Simms, the secretary. She was wearing white stiletto-heeled sandals, the heels digging into the smooth vicarage lawn like tent pegs. 'I never complain,' Mrs Bloxby had said. 'It aerates the lawn.'

'I mean,' went on Miss Simms, 'they've been at each other's throats for years. I think the reason none of them resign is that they don't want to give the others the satisfaction. I'm sorry for you, Mrs Raisin. Sounds like the garden party from hell.'

But James was back in Agatha's mind along with worries about what to wear to dazzle him.

* * *

The day of the garden party was perfect. Clear blue skies and hot sun.

Agatha, in a fine gown of delicately flowered silk and with a wide shady straw hat bedecked with large silk roses, supervised the caterers and took a last look around the garden. Then she went upstairs to check her make-up.

The sound of cars in the lane below her window made her look down. They all seemed to have arrived at once. Mary Owen was wearing a shirtwaister of striped cotton and flat-heeled shoes, and Angela Buckley white cotton trousers and a blue cotton top. Jane Cutler had on a simple Liberty print dress.

Feeling suddenly ridiculously overdressed, Agatha whipped off her hat and gown and put on a cotton skirt and a plain white blouse, and then ran downstairs to meet them.

James was now out in the garden with the caterers. He was wearing faded blue jeans and an open-necked shirt. Agatha realized with a pang that he must have let himself in with the key to her cottage that she had given him in happier times.

She braced herself for her visitors.

The men, Bill Allen, Andy Stiggs and Fred Shaw, as if to make up for the informal dress of the women and James, were all wearing blazers, collars and ties. Bill Allen's blazer had a large gold-embroidered crest on the pocket.

194

Champagne was poured all round. Agatha raised her glass. 'Here's to goodwill,' she said. 'We've all had our differences, but I think we should all be friends.'

'Why?' demanded Mary Owen.

'Because it's more pleasant that way.'

Angela Buckley looked at Agatha suspiciously. 'You don't belong to one of those mad religious sects, do you?'

'I should think it's therapy,' said Mary Owen. 'People who indulge in therapy groups are always wanting chummy get-togethers. Any moment now we'll all have to sit in a circle and talk about the nasty thing that happened to us in the wood-shed all those years ago.'

'That's a good one,' said Bill Allen and gave a great horse-laugh.

'I'm not surprised you go around murdering each other,' said James in a cold, carrying voice.

'Here now. None of that,' said Andy Stiggs, red in the face above a tie which seemed to be strangling him. 'We're all respectable citizens, and if you ask me, that water company's behind these murders.'

'That's what I think,' said Bill Allen.

Muscular Fred Shaw was sweating. 'You lot don't know how to think, that's my opinion. You hated Robina like poison, Mary, and so did you, Angela.'

'I didn't hate her,' said Mary. 'She was one of those dreary little fluffy women of small brain.'

Between the acrimonious exchanges, all were drinking champagne, an efficient waiter making sure all the glasses were kept topped up.

'You and Angela could have learned something about femininity from Robina,' said Fred. 'She was all woman, not a leathery trout like you two.'

'A common little man like you wouldn't know a feminine woman even if she leaped out of your soup and bit you on the bum,' said Angela.

'How do you lot ever get anything done for the parish if you snipe at each other like this?' demanded James. 'Aren't any of you curious to know why Robert Struthers and Robina Toynbee were murdered, and by whom? It could have been one of you.'

There was a shocked silence.

'What's this?' demanded Fred Shaw. 'One of us? Why?'

'Why not?' said Mary Owen. 'You were up at Robina's cottage the evening before she was murdered, Fred. She would have told you about how she planned to make that speech from her garden wall.'

'I'm the only one of you that liked Robina.' Fred wrenched off his tie. Then he took off

196

his blazer and rolled up his shirt sleeves. 'I often went round there, and so did Bill and Andy. It was you and Angela that always had it in for her.'

'Nonsense.' Angela looked at the buffet table. 'Are we going to eat that stuff or not? I'm starving.'

There was a temporary lull while they collected plates of food. Although Agatha had put out chairs in the garden, Angela and Mary sat down on the grass, a sensible move, since it meant they did not have to balance plates of food on their knees. The others joined them.

James began to ask them what they felt about the proposed bypass around Ancombe. Soon Fred Shaw was declaiming it was a disgrace because it would ruin shopkeepers like himself if the through traffic was taken away, and Bill Allen, who ran the garden centre, agreed with him.

'I think it's a good idea,' put in Mary. 'I mean, who wants droves of Americans?'

'What's up with Americans?' demanded Andy Stiggs. 'Damn this tie. You've had the right idea, Fred.' He took his off and then his blazer.

How different the dream always is from the reality, marvelled Agatha. In her dream about the garden party, she stood there gracious in her pretty gown with the lightest of breezes fluttering through the flowers in her hat.

James, in white shirt, blazer and cravat, would be bending over her, smiling in admiration. But James was sitting on the grass with the others, eating cold salmon and drinking champagne and apparently concentrating solely on getting to know these councillors better.

'Oh, these Americans. Everything always so *quaint* and *pretty*. Pah.'

'I thought American-bashing was desperately unfashionable these days,' said Agatha. 'I mean, the ones that get this far are usually pretty sophisticated and seem to know more about the Cotswolds than the locals.'

'So brash and vulgar.' Mary glanced at Agatha. 'Like to like, I suppose.'

'Oh, shut your face and eat your food,' said James, and to Agatha's surprise, Mary laughed and threw him an almost flirtatious look.

'What have you got to do with this water business?' Andy Stiggs asked James.

'It's Agatha's business. I am here to lend her moral support.'

Angela looked narrowly from Agatha to James. Then she said, 'Well, it can't be *romantic* support. Agatha's affair with Guy Freemont is the talk of *both* villages.'

To her fury, Agatha felt herself turning dark red. 'I am not having an affair with Guy Freemont,' she said.

'It's all right, Agatha,' said Mary. 'Angela's

just being catty. Guy Freemont's much too young for you.'

'Listen, the lot of you!' Agatha put her plate and glass carefully on the grass. 'The idea of this garden party was to mend fences, to get you to be friendly towards each other again. It was a great mistake. You're always like this, murder or no murder – nasty, carping, vicious and bitchy. How so many like people should end up on one parish council beats me.'

She stood up and marched into the house and up to her bedroom, where she sat on the edge of her bed and stared bleakly into space. The words about herself and Guy burnt and hurt. Had they not been said in front of James, they would not have mattered much.

Her bedroom door opened and James came quietly in. 'You're a miracle, Agatha.'

'What?' Agatha looked up at him in a dazed way.

'Your outburst has drawn them all together. Come down and sit quietly with me in a corner of the garden and let them get on with it. And listen. They're starting to talk about the murders.'

'James . . .'

But he was already clattering down the stairs. Feeling bruised in spirit, Agatha joined him in the garden. They sat together on the grass, a little way away from the others.

'How much champagne did you order?' asked Agatha. James had said he would take care of the drinks.

'I ordered a bottle a head, but the catering company brought along a lot of extra bottles, which is just as well. They seem to be demolishing rather a lot.'

'It's that waiter. He's never stopped pouring the stuff.'

'I think champagne is rather like your fish and chips, Agatha. Everyone likes the idea but few actually enjoy the taste. Listen!'

'So Robina says to me, just that evening before she was killed.' Fred Shaw was flushed and slightly tipsy. 'She says, "Fred," she says, "I wish to God I had never let them go ahead taking the water." "Why?" asks I. "You was all for it." "Well," she says, says she, "I've been getting these here threatening letters and all I want now is a quiet life."'

'Did she plan to say something like that in her speech?'

'Maybe. I asked the police what was in them typewritten notes but they won't tell me.'

'Better ask Bill Wong,' whispered James.

'Did any of us actually know which way Robert was going to vote?' asked Bill Allen.

A shaking of heads. 'You were close to him, Mary,' said Angela. 'He must have said something.'

Mary shook her head. 'Not to me. Jane?'

All eyes turned to Jane Cutler. She had been relatively quiet since the start of the party. The sun shone on her immaculately groomed hair and on the strange smoothness of her face from which old, suddenly tired eyes looked out.

'He said he liked to keep people guessing. I got quite irritated with him. Said there was no reason for him to go on like the secret service.' She turned to Fred Shaw. 'You said Robina's notes were typewritten. Who told you that?'

'The police.'

'That's odd,' said Jane.

'What's odd? Yes, I will have some more.' Angela held up her glass.

'I never remember Robina having a typewriter. I mean, she was the sort of woman who prided herself on not being able to do anything manual at all. Does anyone remember her having a typewriter?'

There was a shaking of heads.

'She could have got someone to type out her notes for her,' suggested Jane.

'I got the impression from the police they were just notes, not a full typed speech,' said Fred Shaw.

'I don't know why you're all going on about whether her notes were typed or not,' said Angela Buckley. 'I mean, was she murdered because she typed? Ridiculous.'

Fred Shaw's eyes gleamed. 'But don't you see, if she had something in her original *hand-written* notes to say she had changed her mind about the water, someone could have typed out *different* notes to throw us off the scent.'

'And who else would want to do that but the water company?' said Mary Owen. 'I've been against this water business from the start.'

'Oh, we all know *that*,' sneered Angela. 'So much so that you paid a bunch of hoodlums to make trouble. So much for your bloody so-called concern for the environment, Mary *dear*. Bringing louts into the village. They were going to *cement* the spring. *Our* spring, Mary, not just yours!'

'I didn't know what they were really like,' said Mary.

'Oh, yes, you did!' Angela's eyes were blazing. 'You saw damn well what they were like at the first protest, but you kept on paying them.'

'As I told the police, I simply contributed money to what I thought was a worthy cause. I did not know they would demonstrate.'

'Save Our Foxes, Mary? *Save Our Foxes!* Come on. Do the police know you're a member of the Cotswold Hunt?'

'I handed in my resignation a year ago.'

'And told us all it was because you were too old!'

202

'I told you no such thing. I did not think it necessary to explain my reasons to a trollop like you. I saw the error of my ways and contributing to Save Our Foxes was a way of making amends.'

Jane Cutler tittered. 'How odd. I simply cannot imagine you as having one sensitive bone in your body, Mary. You would make a good murderess.'

'Ah, but I have an alibi,' Mary flashed back. 'Which is more than you can say for yourself.'

'The guilty ones always have a cast-iron alibi.'

'Ladies, ladies.' Bill Allen held up his hands, red and powerful in the sunlight. 'Peace. We've all had our differences over the years but we've all stuck together through thick and thin. It's a lovely day and there seems to be a lot more champagne. So let's just bury the hatchet and enjoy ourselves.'

'I'll kill that waiter,' muttered Agatha to James. 'This is going to cost a fortune.'

'Worth every penny. I'll pay for the champers.'

The councillors began to gossip together about safe village topics. Agatha and James seemed to be forgotten.

When they finally all reeled off to their cars, drunkenly oblivious to the fact that each was now well over the limit, James and Agatha waved them goodbye and went in to survey the debris of the party.

'Well, if the purpose of the party had been to really get that nasty lot together again,' said Agatha, 'we succeeded.'

'We got a lot of what we wanted. Let's see if we can get hold of Bill Wong tomorrow and find out more about those notes. And then let's call on Mary's sister. If she's been covering for her, we might be able to guess something from her manner. We need an excuse.'

'I know.' Agatha held up a silver lighter. 'This is Mary's. We can say we happened to be in Mircester and thought she might be visiting.'

Chapter Eight

They drove out under a large, windy Cotswolds sky. The wind had turned cold, a harbinger of autumn. Agatha reflected that the older she got, the shorter got the summers and the longer and darker the winters. Of course, living in the country made a difference. One did not notice winter in the city quite so much.

When they got to police headquarters, it was to find that Bill had a day off and was at home.

'I hate going there,' grumbled Agatha. 'His parents are such downers.'

'Phone first and make sure it's all right,' said James.

Agatha went to a phone-box and dialled Bill's number. Mrs Wong answered.

'Oh, it's you,' she said. 'What do you want?'

'I would like to speak to Bill,' said Agatha patiently.

'Well, you can't –' began Mrs Wong when the phone was taken from her and Bill's voice came on the line.

'We hate to bother you on your day off,' said Agatha.

'We?'

'Me and James. But we wanted to ask you something.'

'Come round. My young lady's here.'

'Oh, in that case, maybe we'd better leave it.'

'No, no. I would really like you to meet her.'

Agatha said they'd be about ten minutes and then rejoined James.

'He says to come round but he's got his young lady there.'

'And is that a problem?' asked James.

'It is, in a way. I'm very fond of Bill and I don't want to be a spectator when his parents ruin his love life one more time.'

'If she really cares for him, then nothing will put her off.'

'Oh, Mrs Wong will think of something.'

They drove to Bill's parents' modern brick house set among others of the same design in a neat private housing estate.

'We're just having a drink before lunch,' said Bill, when he answered the door. 'I'd like to invite you as well, but Mum says she doesn't have enough.'

'It's all right,' said Agatha quickly. 'We'll only be a few minutes.'

'Come into the lounge and meet Sharon and then we'll go out into the back garden for a private chat.'

When they entered the small chilly lounge, the air was heavy with silence. Sharon, a pretty young girl, looked up, her face breaking into a smile of relief.

'Sherry?' offered Bill. He poured two little glassfuls of sweet sherry and handed them to Agatha and James. 'Now this is Sharon Beck. Sharon, Mrs Agatha Raisin and Mr James Lacey.'

'Ever so pleased,' murmured Sharon.

'It's his day off,' grumbled Mr Wong. 'Don't see why people should bother us on Bill's day off.'

'Do you enjoy working at police headquarters?' Agatha asked Sharon.

'Oh, ever so much. The other girls are really nice.'

'Don't hold with girls working once they're married,' said Mr Wong.

There was an awkward silence and then Mrs Wong said, 'It's just as well we've got the spare bedroom.'

Another silence.

'Why?' asked Agatha desperately.

'So that when Bill gets married, they can live here.'

'I didn't think any young married couples lived with the parents of one or the other these days,' said James.

'No reason not to,' said Mrs Wong. 'If Bill marries Sharon here, well, she'll need to stop

207

working because of babies and that, and he doesn't make enough.'

Sharon looked like some frightened animal cowering in the undergrowth.

'I feel awkward breaking into your lunch party.' Agatha stood up. 'If we could just have that word, Bill?'

'Sure. Let's go into the garden.'

'Don't be long,' called Mrs Wong. 'It's shepherd's pie.'

The garden was Bill's domain and its beauty contrasted with the cold stuffiness of his family home.

'So what do you want to know?' he asked.

'Those notes Robina Toynbee left,' said James. 'They were typewritten?'

'Yes.'

'But she didn't have a typewriter,' said Agatha.

'No, we couldn't find one. We're asking around the village to see if she got someone to type them for her.'

'What did the notes say?'

'Not much. Just instructions for the speech. Things like, begin with welcome. Outline benefits to village from water company. That sort of thing. Only two small pages.'

'Don't you find that odd?' asked Agatha. 'I mean, no typewriter?'

'That's what we're looking into.'

'Fred Shaw was up at Robina's cottage the night before,' said James.

'We know.' Bill dead-headed a rose. 'He came forward and told us about it. He said she was being frightened by anonymous letters but she must have burnt them all. We didn't find any.'

'Wait a bit.' Agatha frowned. 'I've just remembered something. Fred Shaw. He was determined to make a speech at the fête himself. I didn't know how to put him off. He said he would call on me and discuss it but he never did.'

'He could have changed his mind when he heard The Pretty Girls were supposed to be opening it.'

'True. But he's very vain and bullying. And there's something else. I can't remember if I told you. There was bad feeling between Andy Stiggs and Robert Struthers. Andy wanted to marry the late Mrs Struthers and claimed Robert had stolen her away.'

'But why kill Robina Toynbee?' asked Bill.

'Because Andy Stiggs was against the water company.'

'Bill!' Mrs Wong, shrill and bad-tempered, appeared in the doorway. 'Are you coming in or not? I was just saying to Sharon that when you're married, she'll need to see you get your meals on time.'

'Coming, Mum.'

'You're not engaged, are you?' asked Agatha.

'Not yet,' said Bill with a grin. 'But that's Mum for you. Always hoping.'

'Yes, that's Mum for you,' said Agatha bitterly as they drove off. 'Can't Bill see how she frightens them all away? But no. He adores his parents and doesn't see anything wrong with them.'

'I suppose, in that, he's luckier than most. Did you adore your parents, Agatha?'

'They were drunk most of the time. I couldn't wait to get away from them. What about you?'

'Mine were great. My father died ten years ago and my mother only survived him by a year. She was devoted to him.'

'What did they die of?'

'My father died of a stroke and my mother of cancer.'

'So much cancer about,' mourned Agatha. 'I must give up smoking.'

'There's a hypnotist in Mircester who's supposed to have a good success rate. There was an article about him in the *Cotswold Journal*. I've still got it.'

'Give it to me when we get back. I'll give it a try.'

'Now can you remember where Mrs Darcy lives?'

'If you go back to the centre I can guide you from there.'

Soon they were cruising along the quiet street where Mary Owen's sister lived. 'Stop here,' said Agatha, 'and we'll get out and walk. I'm not quite sure where it was. It was dark.'

They got out and walked along. 'I think about here.' Agatha stopped. 'There was a street lamp, and yes, a lilac tree.'

'There are several lilac trees along here.'

'Let's try anyway.'

But the woman who answered the door to them was not Mrs Darcy. Mrs Darcy, she volunteered, lived at number 22.

So along to number 22.

Mrs Darcy opened the door and stood looking at them contemptuously. 'Oh, it's you,' she said to Agatha, 'and who's this?'

'Mr James Lacey.'

Mrs Darcy was wearing tortoiseshell-rimmed glasses and a crisp cotton dress and the great likeness to her sister was considerably diminished in the clear light of day. She was slightly shorter in height than her sister.

'What do you want?' she asked.

'We're trying to help clear up these terrible murders,' said James with a charming smile. 'And Mary left her silver lighter at Mrs Raisin's cottage. As we happened to be in Mircester, we thought we would leave it with you.' He handed it over.

'So what have the murders got to do with you? I can understand this woman poking her nose in, but you are obviously a gentleman.'

'I would have thought that you, of all people, would be anxious to see these murders cleared up.'

'Why me?'

'Because Miss Owen is your sister.'

'What's that got to do with it?'

A woman walking her dog paused by the garden gate, listening avidly.

'You'd better come inside,' said Mrs Darcy curtly.

She led the way into a sitting-room, a rather bleak room with green walls and a few dingy oil paintings.

Agatha and James sat side by side on a sofa. Mrs Darcy stood in front of the fireplace.

'So? What's this about Mary?'

'Your sister,' said James patiently, 'paid the Save Our Foxes people to demonstrate.'

'There is no proof of that! Mary's kind-hearted. She was merely contributing to a good cause.'

'I find it hard to believe that Mary cared a damn about foxes, one way or the other,' said Agatha.

'I doubt if you know anything about the countryside at all.' Mrs Darcy turned back to James.

'There's no need to be so rude to Mrs Raisin,' said James sharply. 'In fact, I think the only reason you are being so rude is because you are worried about your sister.'

'I have no reason to worry. You are mistaken. There is nothing I can tell you to help you. On the night Robert Struthers was killed, Mary was here. She had no reason to kill Robina Toynbee. In fact, the suggestion that my sister might have killed anyone is highly insulting. We had dinner together. I did not draw the curtains and several of the neighbours saw us.'

'What time was that?' asked James.

'About sevenish. I do not like eating late.'

'And what time did you both go to bed?'

'About ten. Mary went out to buy milk and newspapers at the corner shop in the morning, and after breakfast she left for Carsely. I would suggest you both leave this matter to the police. Now I would really like to get on . . .'

Outside, Agatha clutched James's arm and said, 'Mary had plenty of time to nip over to Carsely and murder Robert Struthers.'

'I find it hard to believe.' James shook his head. 'Someone could have seen her car in Ancombe.'

'She didn't need to take her own car. She could have taken her sister's. She could have arranged to stay with her sister to establish an alibi.'

James grinned. 'I know you want it to be Mary. But I think we're wasting our time. Let's try Fred Shaw.'

'We could just check at the corner shop and make sure she did buy milk and newspapers.'

'The police will have done that.'

'Still . . .'

'Oh, all right. We'll walk along.'

The corner shop turned out to be one of the last survivors of its kind. Not only did it stock groceries and newspapers, but postcards, gifts, and bags of garden fertilizer.

There was a small wizened man behind the counter. 'We are helping the police with their inquiries,' said James, quickly flashing a credit card in the gloom of the shop.

'I've told the police all I know. Mrs Darcy's sister was in here the morning after that murder. She bought the *Express* and *The Daily Telegraph* and a pint of milk.'

'Are you sure it was Miss Owen?' asked Agatha.

'Yes, she's been in here before. Besides she said something like, "I'm back visiting my sister. I wish she'd do her own shopping."'

'But Miss Owen and Mrs Darcy are very much alike.'

'Mrs Darcy wears glasses. Her sister don't.'

'But what if Mrs Darcy had taken her spectacles off? Would you be able to tell the difference?'

'I s'pose. Miss Owen, she wears trousers all the time and Mrs Darcy wears frocks.'

James tugged at Agatha's arm. 'That will be all. We won't be troubling you further.'

'Don't you see?' said Agatha as they walked back to the car. 'Mrs Darcy could have been covering for her sister. We'd better tell Bill.'

'You know what I think?' said James gloomily. 'I think that shopkeeper will tell Mrs Darcy of our visit and that she will complain to the police and I will get a lecture for impersonating a detective or something.'

'Surely not.'

'Surely yes. That shopkeeper will tell his other customers that we practically accused Mrs Darcy of covering for her sister. I hope we don't end up in court. In fact, we'd better go and tell Bill.'

Bill Wong listened to them, his face darkening.

'You've gone too far this time,' he said. 'If she makes a complaint, I can't protect you. Just leave it alone now. I should not have encouraged you.'

'But we did find out something for you,' pleaded Agatha.

'No, you have done a bad thing. I cannot do anything to limit the damage. Let's just hope we hear no more about it.'

'Now, where?' asked Agatha as they stood in the car park outside the police headquarters.

'Fred Shaw?'

'I feel small,' said Agatha wearily. 'I feel I've just been ticked off by the teacher. I feel I'm a bad person. I'll tell you, James, I have never been so insulted by so many people as I have been since the first murder took place.'

'Oh, you're all right,' said James absent-mindedly. 'Let's see Fred.'

They drove out of Mircester. It was the end of August. A few leaves were already turning yellow and there was a faint chill in the air. Agatha began to feel that every winter in the country with its fogs and icy roads was another little death. She could take a holiday somewhere sunny and miss the bad weather and the frantic ho-ho-ho jollity of Christmas, but the fact was she was increasingly reluctant to leave her cats. When they die, she vowed, I'll never keep another animal. It was no fun going away any more when part of her heart was always worrying if they were all right.

Her thoughts turned to Guy. He had at least given her a buzz when she was out with him, although the look-what-*I've*-got feeling was mitigated by the feeling that people might think her too old for him.

And what of James? Driving so competently, seemingly unfazed by the fact that they might both soon be in deep trouble. He would probably take himself off, she thought bitterly, and leave her alone to face the music.

She no longer knew what she felt for him. Relationships had to move forward, even an inch, or, like one of those videos she rented, the film came to an end and the tape began to run backwards – only, in her mind, showing not the happy scenes, but a long list of rejections.

She would see this case to the end, if it ever ended, and then detach herself from him.

They drove into Ancombe and stopped outside Fred Shaw's shop. He was serving a customer. He looked down the shop and saw them. 'Be with you shortly,' he called.

He served his customer with four batteries, said goodbye, and then approached them.

'What do you want?' he asked truculently.

'Just a few questions,' said James.

'I'm shutting the place up for lunchtime,' he said. 'Come into the back shop.'

He locked the door and pulled down the blind. He jerked his head and they followed him into the back shop.

'So what do you want?' There was no offer of whisky this time.

'We feel that life in Ancombe will never really go back to normal until these murders have been solved,' began James.

'So what's that got to do with me? The police are working on it.'

'Yes, but you are a man of business, a shrewd man,' said Agatha quickly.

The truculence left Fred's face. 'I do see a lot of things other people don't,' he said in a mollified voice.

'I heard something about Andy Stiggs being in love with Mrs Struthers. Mrs Struthers must have been younger than her husband.'

'Yes, she was. Andy also thought he should have been chairman of the council as well. He will be now.'

'Do you think he could have murdered Robina as well?' asked Agatha.

'Here now. I never said he murdered Robert. But he was always around Robina's. Maybe he saw something.'

'As Andy Stiggs was against the water company, that must have soured his relations with Robina,' said Agatha.

'I think he thought he could persuade her to change her mind.'

Agatha looked at him thoughtfully, wondering when she could slip in a question about his speech. Instead she said, 'Was there ever a Mrs Stiggs?'

'Yes, he married Ethel Fairweather on the

rebound right after Robert got married and lived unhappily right up until her death. She was a shrew. In some way, he blamed Robert for his rotten marriage, know what I mean?'

'Where does he live?' asked James. 'I have his address but I'm not sure exactly where his cottage is.'

'Second on the left past the church.'

'You never called to see me with your speech,' said Agatha.

'What speech?'

'The one you were going to make at the fête.'

'When I heard that pop group was coming, I knew you wouldn't want me.'

And yet the pop group was a relatively late booking, thought Agatha. And when Fred had thought that Jane Harris was to open the fête, it had not stopped him.

'You don't think Mary Owen could have had anything to do with it?' asked Agatha. 'I mean, it turns out as far as I can gather that she's not broke after all. She paid those protesters.'

'She's big enough, strong enough and nasty enough,' said Fred. 'But Andy Stiggs is my choice.'

'You thought it was Mary Owen at one time.'

'Did I? I can't remember that.'

'So let's try Andy Stiggs,' said James when they left the shop.

'What's our approach?'

'Same as with Fred. Just want to get it cleared up.'

Andy Stiggs's cottage was a mellow building of Cotswold stone with a newly thatched roof. There was a pleasing jumble of old-fashioned flowers: stocks, impatiens, delphiniums, lupins, and roses, roses all the way.

Andy Stiggs was weeding a flowerbed. He straightened up as they came through the garden gate.

'What?' he demanded.

Oh, to be from the police and be able to say, 'Just a few questions,' with an air of authority, thought Agatha.

'We were in the village,' said James, 'and we thought we would drop in and see you.'

'Why?' He brushed earth from his large hands.

'As vice-chairman of the council, soon to be chairman, you must know a lot about what goes on in the village.'

'And what's that got to do with you? You don't live here.'

'You surely want these murders cleared up.'

'Of course I do, and the answer is staring you in the face. It's that water company. It's my belief that poor Robina changed her mind and so they bumped her off.'

'I think it's only on TV that companies go around bumping people off,' said Agatha.

'*You* can't see what's under your nose because that Guy Freemont has been romancing you,' said Andy.

'That's got nothing to do with it!' Agatha's face flamed.

'To my mind it has. What else would a young man like that be doing with a woman of your age?'

'That's enough of that,' said James coldly. 'You are just as suspect. I gather that Robert Struthers pinched the love of your life from under your nose.'

'That was years and years ago.'

'Sometimes resentments grow with the passing of time.'

Andy picked up a hoe and brandished it at them. 'Get out of here. Just get out and don't come round again or I'll . . .'

'Or I'll what?' asked James. 'Murder us? Come along, Agatha.'

'I think I've got a headache coming on,' said Agatha as they walked back to the car. 'If you don't mind, I would like to go home and lie down for a little.'

'I think we've done enough for one day anyway,' said James.

Half an hour later, Agatha crawled under the duvet on her bed and drew her knees up to her chin. She felt she could not go on investigating the murders. The council members with their insults had finally been able to intimidate her.

Despite the warmth of the duvet and the warmth of the day, she shivered. All the Carsely security, all the safety, all the comfort seemed to have been ripped away and she was alone once more in a hostile world.

The phone rang, loudly and imperatively. She heaved herself up on one elbow and looked at it. What if it was James? No, probably Roy trying to get her back into PR, or something like that. Let it ring and she would check the answering service in a few minutes and find out who had called.

She waited and then dialled 1571. 'There is one message,' said the prissy voice. 'Would you like to hear it?'

'Yes,' muttered Agatha.

'I am afraid I didn't quite get that. Would you like to hear your message?'

'Yes!' shouted Agatha, exasperated.

She waited. Then a harsh voice said, 'This is Mary Owen. Come and see me as soon as possible.'

Oh, dear, thought Agatha bleakly. She's heard about us questioning the corner shop. I'd better get James.

But there was no reply. Agatha climbed out of bed and washed and dressed. She suddenly did not want to wait for James. She wanted to get it over and done with.

She drove steadily to the manor-house in Ancombe, wondering all the while if Mary meant to take her to court for harassment or invasion of privacy or something.

Mary answered the door. 'Follow me,' she said curtly. She led the way into a dark drawing-room: beamed ceiling, thick curtains, stuffed creatures in glass cases, a brass urn of pampas-grass, a drawing-room out of a Hammer horror movie.

'Sit down,' barked Mary.

'I'd rather stand.' Agatha felt she might have to make a quick getaway

'Very well. You have been spreading scandal in my sister's neighbourhood, questioning her local shopkeeper. If you do anything like that again, a nasty accident could happen to you.'

Mary had walked up close to Agatha as she said this. Agatha took a step backwards.

'We were just trying to clear up loose ends,' she protested. 'If you are innocent, you have nothing to fear.'

'Just who the hell do you think you are?' She grabbed Agatha by the shoulder and pulled her towards a large mirror over the fireplace. 'Look at yourself! You are a middle-aged woman and no lady. You poke your nose into things that don't concern you.' She gave Agatha another shove. 'Just get out of here and remember: Any more interference and I'll come looking for you!'

Thoroughly demoralized, Agatha stumbled for the door. She drove off, not even looking in the driving mirror to see if Mary was watching her. She never wanted to see her again.

She was getting out of her car outside her cottage when Mrs Darry came scuttling along, the small bundle of yapping hair which passed for a dog trotting in front of her.

'Mrs Raisin!' she called.

Darry, Darcy, bitches all, thought Agatha, and whipping out her keys, let herself into her cottage and slammed the door.

She leaned her back against the door and breathed deeply.

The doorbell rang. 'Go away!' shrieked Agatha.

'Are you all right, dear?' The voice of Mrs Bloxby came faintly from the other side.

Agatha opened the door and promptly burst into tears.

'Oh, come along into the kitchen,' said Mrs Bloxby, putting an arm around Agatha's shaking shoulders.

Rubbing her eyes on the back of her sleeve, Agatha allowed herself to be led through to her kitchen and gently thrust down into a chair.

'I'll make some strong sweet tea,' said the vicar's wife, plugging in the electric kettle and then handing Agatha the box of tissues which had been lying on the kitchen counter.

Agatha blew her nose and said weakly, 'I'm sorry. Everything got too much for me.'

'Wait until I make us some tea and you can tell me all about it.'

Soon, with her hands wrapped around a mug of tea, Agatha poured out everything, about her shame at her affair with Guy, about not knowing where she stood with James, and finally about the threat from Mary Owen.

'That's very interesting,' said Mrs Bloxby. 'About Mary Owen.'

'Do you mean if she could threaten me, she could have murdered them?'

'Not exactly. If Mary Owen and her sister were the straight and outraged people they claim to be, why did they not complain to the police?'

'Maybe they did.'

'Can you find out?'

'Wait a minute. I'll try to get Bill.'

To Agatha's relief, Bill Wong was at police headquarters.

'What is it now, Agatha?' he asked sharply. 'What have you been up to?'

Agatha told him about Mary's threat and then said, 'Has either Mary or her sister complained to the police about me and James?'

'No, thank goodness.'

'Don't you see, that's what so odd about it? If she and her sister were as innocent as they claim to be, they'd simply have gone to the police.'

There was a silence. Then Bill said slowly, 'But you are making a complaint about Mary Owen threatening you.'

'I don't know, Bill. No witnesses. But she phoned and left a message on my answering service asking me to come and see her.'

'Do you still have that message?'

'Yes.'

'Keep it. I'd like to listen to it. But I'll go and have a talk to her.'

'Are you sure she isn't in need of money, Bill?'

'Oh, that. No, we checked her bank statements. She's pretty wealthy.'

'So why did Fred Shaw say she wasn't?'

'I asked him. He said since she did all the gardening and cleaning herself, with only a bit of occasional help, he assumed she had gone broke. Leave it to me.'

He rang off. Agatha rejoined Mrs Bloxby in the kitchen. 'Neither Mary nor her sister complained to the police.'

'Very odd, that,' said Mrs Bloxby. 'I don't like to see you so distressed.'

'It's all the insults and cracks about my affair with Guy. I've been made to feel like a vulgar trollop.'

'You must not take it all to heart. The fact is that you are dealing with a lot of frightened people. Everyone is suspect and they know it and so they take their fright out on you because they see you as some enemy stirring up the muddy waters.'

'I hadn't thought of it that way. I slammed the door in Mrs Darry's face before you came. She's a horror.'

'I'm afraid she is. Cheer up. She whines that she is very disappointed in Carsely and that it is not a very nice place at all. I feel she will be leaving us soon.'

'I do hope so. That woman has halitosis of the soul.'

After Mrs Bloxby had left, Agatha went up-stairs and washed her face and put on make-up. She would call on James and tell him about Mary. If only he would put his arms about her and hold her close.

Bracing herself, she went next door and rang his bell.

James answered the door, looking flustered. 'What is it, Agatha?'

'Aren't you going to ask me in?'

'I'm actually very busy packing.'

'Where are you going?'

'I'm going up to London for a few days.'

'Why?'

'Private business.'

Agatha felt so rejected, so forlorn, that she did not tell him about Mary. 'Bye,' she said weakly and walked away.

James looked after her impatiently, at the droop of her shoulders. He opened his mouth to call her back and then shut it again and went back inside to finish his packing.

Agatha, in her own cottage, dialled Roy's office. She didn't want to be alone. Roy would surely come running if she asked him.

Roy came on the phone. 'Changed your mind about the water company, Aggie?'

'What?'

'I mean, are you going to go on working for them after all?'

'No.'

'So is this just a friendly chat?'

'I wondered whether you would like to come down for the weekend?'

Roy had been invited to a barbecue on Saturday by his boss and he was not going to turn down such an important invitation, particularly as the boss had a marriageable daughter.

'Sorry, sweetie, too busy. Maybe another time.'

'Yes. Bye.'

Agatha sat staring at the phone. She wondered if she should pack a suitcase herself, drive to Heathrow and get on the first available plane out to anywhere.

The phone rang. Agatha picked it up cautiously, as if the receiver might bite.

'Agatha!' It was Guy's voice. 'I really miss you. What about dinner on Saturday?'

'I don't know . . .'

'Come on. It would be nice to see you again. That French restaurant in Mircester. What about it? I could pick you up at eight.'

'All right,' said Agatha, thinking as she said goodbye and replaced the receiver, what the hell, nobody else wants me.

By Friday, Agatha was feeling calmer. Some healthy walks and a comfortable meeting of the Carsely Ladies' Society did much to restore her equanimity, that and the news that Mrs Darry had gone on holiday.

By late on Friday evening she had decided to cancel her date with Guy. She was just reaching for the phone when it rang. She picked it up gingerly, all her old fears coming back.

'This is Portia Salmond,' said a cool voice. 'I think we should talk.'

'So talk.'

'I don't want to talk over the phone. Can you come here?'

'Where's here?'

'I live at 5 Glebe Street. It's near the abbey in Mircester.'

'I know it. Why now? It's late.'

'It won't take long.'

Curiosity overcame Agatha. 'Give me half an hour.'

She drove through the quiet night-time lanes and then down the A44 to the Fosse. There was a chill in the air. Summer had gone.

She wondered if James had ever taken Portia out for dinner. That was what she really wanted to find out.

Glebe Street was narrow and cobbled and dark. A sliver of moon hung in the sky at the end of the street and the great bulk of the abbey loomed over the houses on the left.

Great English abbeys and minsters always reminded Agatha more of the power of the state, the crown and the army than the power of God.

She parked the car. Number 5 was a trim little house, like a mews house.

The lights were on behind the windows.

Agatha knocked on the pretentious brass knocker in the shape of a grinning demon.

There was a clack of high heels from the other side of the door and then Portia opened it, the light from the hall shining on her blonde hair.

'Come in, Mrs Raisin.'

She led the way into a small living-room done in shades of green: green carpet, green-and-gold curtains, green linen-fabric upholstery on the sofa and two armchairs. On the walls were various photographs of Portia.

'Sit down,' said Portia abruptly. 'I want to get this over with.'

'Okay. Let's have it.'

'I am having an affair with Guy Freemont,' said Portia.

'Really?' Agatha wondered why she didn't feel more surprised.

'Yes, really. He is only amusing himself with you. I think he's got a mother complex. I want you to back off.'

'Are you engaged, married?'

'No.'

'Then what's it got to do with you, sweetheart?'

'You are making a laughing-stock of yourself. Everyone is laughing at you. Someone at the office said the other day, "Who's that old woman I saw with Guy the other night? His mother?"'

Agatha stood up. Her legs felt like lead. She felt unutterably weary. She looked down at Portia.

'Get stuffed, you dreary bag,' said Agatha. 'Get double stuffed. And you think you could do my job in public relations? Well, you can't sleep your way into column inches. It's been tried by sluts like you and it doesn't work. Don't ever phone me or speak to me again.'

She marched to the door. Portia followed her and caught her arm. 'He's seeing you for dinner tomorrow. Don't go!'

'Get *off!*' Agatha rammed her elbow into Portia's ribs, jerked open the door and unlocked her car.

'I'm warning you!' screamed Portia.

'Join the queue, darling.' Agatha got into the car and drove off, her hands damp on the steering-wheel. This case had been too much for her. But she was going on that date with Guy. That blonde bitch was not going to tell such as Agatha Raisin what she could or could not do!

Chapter Nine

The following morning, Bill Wong called on Agatha. He looked depressed and weary.

'How did you get on with Mary Owen?' asked Agatha.

'She denied everything. She said your accusation was fantastic and she thought you deranged. I won't repeat the rest of the insults.'

'This case is getting you down.'

'It's not just the case, Agatha. It's Sharon.'

'Oh.'

'At first she said she couldn't go out with me because her mother was visiting or her hair needed washing or things like that, so I asked her straight out if we were finished and she said yes. I don't know what happened. We were getting on so well together.'

Agatha took a deep breath. 'Bill, do you think your mother frightened her off?'

'Mum? How?'

'Well, by talking about marriage and about Sharon and you living with them.'

'Why would that frighten her off?'

'Bill, no woman wants to live with the in-laws, no matter how nice they are.'

'But Sharon would have said something.'

'Not necessarily. You hadn't even proposed to her. She might think she was being hustled towards marriage.'

He buried his hands in his thick dark hair. 'I never thought of that.'

Agatha shook her head. Bill was highly intelligent when it came to police work but when it came to dealing with women, he was as thick as two planks.

'Anyway, enough of my love life. What about yours?'

'A mess. James has taken off again and I think it's because he anticipated trouble from Mary Owen and her sister, so he cleared off, leaving me to deal with any trouble on my own.'

'That doesn't sound like James.'

'That's very like James. He did the same thing to me in Cyprus. So I'm seeing Guy Freemont this evening and now I don't really want to see him. It was Portia warning me off . . .'

'Portia? Portia Salmond, the secretary?'

'The same. She said she was having an affair with Guy.'

'Messy. Do you really fancy Guy?'

Agatha sighed. 'Only when my ego is battered, as it is now. I'm flattered that a younger man, a handsome man, should want my company. But I don't think I want to be seen out with him, I feel so battered. I think I'll run over to Marks and Spencer in Cheltenham and get something and have a meal here.'

'Hasn't he booked a table at some restaurant?'

'If he has, he can cancel it. I want peace and privacy to tell him that the affair is over.'

'So you *were* having an affair!'

'Does that shock you?'

'No. No I suppose not. I suppose it's because we're friends, I never think of you in that way.' Bill laughed. 'Rather like finding out one's mother is having an affair.'

A picture of Bill's sour mother rose before Agatha's eyes. She wondered whether it would not be better to forget about love and romance, to forget about dieting and the beautician and get fat and frumpy and wear large tentlike dresses and eat everything smothered in double cream.

She suddenly wished that Roy would change his mind and come down. She would cancel her date and they would both go out on an eating binge.

'Ever find that cat?'

'No, no white Persians anywhere.'

Agatha rested her chin on her hands. 'I've been thinking about all of them, the parish councillors. At first it seemed incredible that any one of such a bunch of worthy citizens should commit murder, but once you start scraping below the surface, there's all these resentments and jealousies and passions. Find out anything about where Robina got her notes typed?'

'No, we've hit a dead end on that one as well.'

'I'm really beginning to think it was Andy Stiggs.'

'The vice-chairman. Why him?'

'He seems a violent man. He had a life-long resentment against Robert Struthers because Struthers married the love of his life and Andy married a shrew on the rebound and blamed Robert for that. Then he really hated the idea of the water company, and furthermore he thought he ought to have been chairman.'

'We've got nothing on him. That's the trouble with this lot. There's nothing in any of their backgrounds that points to the character of a murderer.'

'There is Mary Owen, however, paying that group to make trouble.'

'She's certainly a nasty piece of work.'

'They're all nasty,' said Agatha. 'In fact, I have endured so many threats and insults that you'll be glad to learn that I am not going to do any more investigating.'

'Now, that's sensible, Agatha. The police may seem to be moving very slowly, but we're thorough and we'll get there in the end. Although I must admit I'm tired and I'm taking the rest of the day off.'

Agatha drove into Cheltenham and bought food for dinner: salmon mousse for a starter, duckling in orange sauce – check the packet to make sure it could go in the microwave – and sticky toffee pudding. She also bought some microwavable vegetables and a packet of potatoes in a cheese sauce. She wasn't quite sure whether potatoes au gratin went with duckling in orange sauce, but she did not feel like buying real ones.

She then loaded the groceries in her car and walked back along the Promenade, looking in the expensive boutiques, hoping to spy some dress which would miraculously take years off her, but without success.

When she returned home, she put the packets of food in the fridge and went upstairs to lie down for an hour and read. But she fell fast asleep, not waking until six in the evening.

She awoke with a start and let out a faint scream when she saw the time on her bedside clock. She went downstairs to lay the table in the dining-room and to vacuum the sitting-room and set the fire ready to be lit.

Then she went upstairs again and had a bath and began to search through her stock of clothes for something elegant but comfortable to wear. She finally found a long purple caftan with gold embroidery which she hadn't worn in years. It would do. It was loose and comfortable and yet looked like a dinner gown.

She then made up her face carefully and brushed her hair till it shone.

Agatha was about to rise from the dressing-table when she gave an exclamation of irritation. The clothes she had been wearing the day before were thrown in a heap in the corner of the room. It was not as if she expected Guy to see the inside of her bedroom again, but still, they ought to be in the laundry basket.

She picked up her underwear and a navy blouse. She tossed the lot into the laundry basket. Then in the bright light of the bathroom – one-hundred-watt bulb, all the better to see you with – she stared down into the laundry.

She gingerly picked up the navy blouse. There, on the back of it, were several white hairs. Surely they were cat hairs!

She ran into the bedroom and found the skirt she had been wearing. Two white hairs clung to the skirt.

She sat down suddenly on the bed. Mary Owen. It must have been Mary Owen.

But she had a sudden vivid picture of Mary Owen barking, 'Sit down,' and she had refused. Certainly Mary had come up close to her when she had shoved her in front of the mirror.

Then another picture came into her mind. Portia. And she had sat on Portia's sofa while Portia had sneered at her.

She must phone Bill. He had said he was taking the rest of the day off. She got her personal phone book and dialled his number.

'What is it?' demanded a cross voice on the other end of the line. Mrs Wong.

'This is Agatha Raisin and I must speak to Bill immediately.'

'He's in the bath and I'm not getting him.'

Agatha took a deep breath. 'I'm phoning to tell him Sharon is pregnant.'

There was a gasp and then the sound of retreating footsteps. Agatha hung on grimly.

'Rubbish,' she heard Bill saying. 'She's joking.' Then his voice came on the phone.

'What the hell are you up to, Agatha? You've nearly given Mum a heart attack.'

'Bill, listen! I had to get you to the phone. The clothes I was wearing to Portia's last night. They've got *white cat hairs* on them.'

'We never even thought of her,' said Bill. 'I'll get on to it right away. Good work.'

For once Bill ignored his mother's questions and doggedly got dressed. He was just about to go out when the phone rang again. He seized the receiver before his mother could get to it. 'James Lacey,' said the hurried voice at the other end. 'Listen!'

Bill listened. Then he said, 'Christ. And he's at Agatha's tonight!'

Earlier that day, James had taken an old friend to lunch in the City. They talked of old times and at last James felt he had had enough of the courtesies and asked abruptly, 'Did you find out anything about the Freemont brothers?'

His friend, Johnny Birrell, said, 'I asked about and dug about. They borrowed very heavily from the banks to fund this water company.'

'So they didn't come out of Hong Kong very rich? I suppose I'm naïve, I thought every businessman came out of Hong Kong very rich.'

'Not all,' said Johnny. 'I was over there for a couple of years myself. There was one rumour about Guy Freemont you might like to hear.'

'Anything.'

'Right. They were in the clothes business, ran sweatshops, got them into trouble here but not in Hong Kong. But their business was doing well. Then they hit a snag. It's all whispers, of course.'

'What? What did people say?'

'The rumour was that Guy was crazy about this Chinese girl and she did lead him on a bit, but then turned him down. It was said he raped her. Now this Guy Freemont thought no more about it. The girl was only Chinese. Chaps like Guy Freemont can think they're in love with a girl without respecting her one bit. But the girl's father was a very rich and powerful Chinese businessman. Evidently there was no proof other than the girl's word that Guy had raped her, and she had been fooling about with several men. But whatever happened, or whatever threats were laid on Guy, I don't exactly know, but the rumour is that he and his brother had to practically bankrupt themselves to buy Guy's way out of trouble. This was right before the Chinese took over. Mind you, it could all be exaggerated. You know what ex-pat communities are like, James. One gets hold of a story and embroiders it and then the other adds to it and passes it on.'

James rose to his feet, glancing at his watch. 'I'll pay for this and run, Johnny. I must get back to the country as soon as possible.'

But on the road back, James began to wish he were one of those mobile-phone users he so despised. His car, which had served him so well, came to a stop and refused to move. A motorist stopped and allowed James to use his mobile phone. Then James had to wait for the breakdown truck. Because his car was causing a bottleneck in the traffic, the breakdown man suggested he tow it straight to the garage and examine it there.

James went dark red with embarrassment in the garage when a laughing mechanic pointed out that all that was up with the car was that it had run out of petrol.

By the time James was able to phone Bill, the sun was setting, and he considered he had been panicking. He had found out Guy Freemont was probably a shifty businessman and a rapist, but that didn't make him a murderer. Anyway, he thought sourly, he didn't have to rape Agatha to get what he wanted.

But when he heard the anxiety in Bill's voice and that she was actually entertaining Guy Freemont, all his worries came flooding back. 'Don't phone Agatha,' Bill warned. 'If he's guilty, we don't want him alerted. I haven't time to tell you the rest; I'm on my way there.'

Agatha went to answer the door and let Guy in. 'Is it raining?' she asked, noticing wet drops glittering on his coat.

'Just started. Are you ready?'

'I thought we would eat here,' said Agatha. 'Let me take your coat.'

She helped him out of it and went to hang it in the hall closet. Her mind had been numb since she phoned Bill. All she could keep wondering was why, if it had been Portia all along, had she done it? She must be some sort of maniac. Should she tell Guy?

But as she slowly put the coat away, Agatha at last was struck by a blinding flash of the obvious. Guy was having an affair with Portia. Guy would have been at Portia's house. Guy could have got cat hairs on his clothes and transferred one to Robert Struthers's clothes. How many people had shouted at her that the Freemonts were guilty and she, the great PR, had refused to believe them? You don't murder for publicity, or do you?

She had better phone Bill. But Bill would be checking Portia, and if she had a Persian cat and was innocent, then they would focus their attention on Guy and, thank God, she had told Bill that Guy Freemont was coming to her house.

Agatha went slowly into the sitting-room and put a match to the fire and then stood looking down at the flames.

'Aren't you going to offer me a drink?' Guy's voice came from behind her.

She gave a little start. 'Sorry, I was daydreaming. Whisky?'

'Yes, please. Just a splash of soda.'

Agatha gave him a generous whisky and soda and poured herself a gin and tonic.

243

'I'm glad you decided to see me, Agatha,' said Guy. 'I thought you had dropped me.'

'Oh, we were never really an item,' said Agatha. She must play for time. If Bill found that cat and if it were all connected to Guy, then the police would arrive in force.

'I thought we were.'

'That's odd. Portia Salmond summoned me last night and told me you had been having an affair with her.'

'Agatha, Agatha. That was all a long time ago.'

'Can't have been. The water company's pretty new. You only hired Portia this year.'

'I knew her before.'

'In Hong Kong?'

His eyes narrowed. 'Been checking up on me, Agatha?'

'Of course. When I was approached to represent your company, I asked a few questions about your background.'

'And what did my busy little angel find out?'

'I found out you'd been in the rag trade and had moved back here when Hong Kong went over to the Chinese. Dreadful for those poor people in Hong Kong. They should all have been given British passports.'

'Come on, Agatha. They're Chinese, too.'

'So? They're people and they were British subjects.'

He shook his handsome head. 'I never took you for a liberal.'

'You mean the wogs begin at Calais?'

'Let's drop this. So boring. So you are a retired lady of leisure?'

'Yes, and I plan to enjoy it. How's the water business?'

'We are doing so well. Exporting to Europe and soon to America. And all thanks to the publicity.'

'I'll never understand that. When I see a bottle of Ancombe Water with the skull grinning on the label, all I can think of is poor Mr Struthers lying at the well and the water stained with his blood swirling around the basin.'

'Don't you see, Agatha? That's the secret.'

'The secret of what?'

'Advertising, promoting a product. There's a new health drink on sale which has a cannabis leaf on the label. Now it doesn't contain the drug-type hash because the cannabis in it is from the male leaf and it's only the female leaf which causes a high. Do you think people buy it because they think it'll be healthy? No, they think, Maybe I'll get a high.'

'I'm still not with you. There's nothing in Ancombe Water but water, surely.'

'I discussed this with you before. All human beings are self-destructive. A lot of people go into health shops to buy stuff that will pep them up or slow them down but persuade themselves that as they are buying whatever in a *health* shop, it makes it all right. People will sozzle their brains in pubs with alcohol and sneer about junkies. Vegetarians stuff their faces with sugar. And in my opinion the health warning on a packet of cigarettes is one of the best advertisements going. People are drawn to death, Agatha, because of their fear of it, like people are drawn to the edge of a cliff. And never have people been more afraid of death than in this age.'

'I can't really go along with that,' said Agatha. 'People have very short memories. Ancombe Water was flashed around the world because of the murders, yes. But then they forget that and just remember they've heard about it. I don't believe that dicing with death has any attraction at all.' Agatha lit a cigarette.

Guy pulled a newspaper cutting out of his pocket. 'Oh, yes? Well, I've brought you a cutting about a hypnotist in Mircester. You do want to stop smoking, don't you?'

'Yes,' lied Agatha, who did not really in her heart want to stop at all. 'I'll get you another drink and then I'll fix dinner.'

'Okay. I'll join you in the kitchen.'

'No, don't do that. I don't like anyone watching me cooking.'

She gave him another drink and then went into the kitchen and shut the door. All that talk about death being good for publicity. Was it Guy after all who was the murderer? She had arranged the salmon mousse on plates. The duck would need to be heated in the microwave and then both portions, along with the already microwaved potatoes and vegetables, kept warm in the oven.

What a fool she had been! James had kept insisting it was the Freemonts. How James would crow over her.

She looked back at the closed kitchen door. Maybe a call to police headquarters . . .

She cautiously picked up the receiver and got through to police headquarters. She asked for Bill but was told he was out. 'Tell him,' she said urgently, 'that Guy Freemont is at my home and I am convinced he committed those murders. This is Mrs Agatha Raisin. No, I haven't time to wait to be put through to anyone else . . .' She heard a movement outside the kitchen door and quickly replaced the receiver.

Her cats curled around her legs. She opened the kitchen door and shooed them out into the garden. 'You'll be safe there,' she whispered, and was later to wonder why she had not run out of the kitchen door and fled to safety herself.

She put the duckling in the microwave, picked up the two plates of salmon mousse and headed for the dining-room.

She put down the plates and lit the candles. Then she went through to the sitting-room.

'Were you on the phone?' asked Guy. He was standing by the fireplace.

'Were you listening?' asked Agatha lightly.

'No, when you pick up the receiver in the kitchen, the receiver in here gives a little ping.'

'Yes, I was on the phone. I was calling Mrs Bloxby, the vicar's wife.'

His face was hard and his eyes glittered oddly in the firelight. He took a step towards her.

The doorbell rang.

The police, thought Agatha.

'I'll just get that.'

He caught hold of her arm. 'Don't you want to be alone with me?'

He studied her face. Agatha tried to look as puzzled and offended as she would have been in normal circumstances.

'All right,' he said, releasing her.

Agatha went to the door and opened it. Mrs Bloxby stood on the doorstep.

Agatha goggled at her and then raised her voice. 'I was just saying to Guy when I phoned you a moment ago that it was bound to be you.' She winked desperately.

'I brought you some of my trifle.' Mrs Bloxby held out a bowl.

'Come in and meet Guy,' said Agatha.

248

'If you're entertaining, I don't want to interrupt you.'

'Just a drink,' pleaded Agatha.

'Yes, how nice.' Guy loomed up behind Agatha.

'How good to see you, Mr Freemont,' said Mrs Bloxby. 'I won't stay long. As I was saying to Agatha a moment ago on the phone, I thought she might like some of my special trifle.'

Guy looked as relaxed now as he had been tense a moment before. 'You take the trifle, Agatha, and I'll get Mrs Bloxby a drink.' Mrs Bloxby handed over the bowl of trifle and then put her umbrella in the stand in the hall.

'Such a dreadful evening, Mr Freemont,' she said. 'Oh, this is comfortable. I always think a log fire is so pretty. Just a sherry, please.'

Agatha came in and sat down. The fact that Guy was more than likely a cold-blooded killer had finally sunk in and she felt sick and frightened.

Mrs Bloxby looked brightly at Agatha and then at Guy. 'Do you go to church, Mr Freemont?'

'What?

'I asked, do you go to church?'

'Why?'

'Because I am the vicar's wife and I like to collect as many souls for the church as possible.'

Mrs Bloxby knows, thought Agatha. Somehow she knows. It was totally out of character for the vicar's wife to ask anyone if they went to church.

Guy gave an awkward laugh. 'Well, Christmas, Easter; I'm afraid I am a two-service-a-year Anglican.'

'But are you never afraid for your immortal soul?'

'Never think about it.'

'Oh, but you should. We will all be judged on Judgement Day.'

'I don't want to offend you, Mrs Bloxby, but it's all a lot of tosh. When someone dies, they just die – finish, the end.'

'That is where you are wrong.'

'How do you know that? God tell you so?'

Mrs Bloxby took a sip of sherry and looked meditatively at the leaping flames. 'No, but I have observed goodness in people as well as evil. There is a bit of the divine spirit in all of us. I have also observed an odd pattern of justice.'

'Justice?' demanded Guy sharply and Agatha groaned inwardly.

'Oh, yes, I have seen evil people thinking they have got away with things, but they always suffer in the end.'

'The fires of hell?'

'Yes, and they suffer from them in their lifetime. I think whoever killed poor Mr Struthers and Robina Toynbee will eventually suffer dreadfully.'

'Not if the police don't catch him, or her.' Guy stood up. 'Excuse me, I've left my cigarettes in my coat pocket.'

'Have one of mine,' said Agatha. 'I didn't know you smoked.'

'There's a lot about me you don't know.'

He went out. Agatha looked at the vicar's wife with agonized eyes. She mouthed, 'Don't go too far.'

Guy came in and stood in the doorway. He had his coat on and a small serviceable revolver was pointed straight at them.

'Fun's over,' he said coldly. 'We're going for a ride. Into the car and one squeak and I'll shoot both of you.'

'Why are you doing this?' demanded Agatha.

'Just shut up and get moving. Move!'

Outside, he snarled at Agatha. 'You drive and the Holy Roller can sit beside you. One false move and I'll kill you both.'

'Take the road through Ancombe,' he ordered as Agatha drove off.

Agatha felt all hope die. The police would come into the village the other way and so miss them. The cold muzzle of the revolver was pressed against her neck.

Mrs Bloxby sat quietly beside her, hands

clasped in prayer. What good will that do? Agatha wanted to scream at her.

'Down to Moreton and take the Fosse towards Stratford,' ordered Guy.

Agatha obeyed. There was nothing else she could do. Jammed beside her on the seat was her handbag, which she had picked up through force of habit. Was there anything in it she could use as a weapon? Nail scissors? Forget it. There was a little can of spray lacquer. If only she could get that and spray it in his face. But how?

Start him talking, she thought. 'So you killed them?' she said.

'Just drive and keep your mouth shut.'

In books, thought Agatha wildly, the criminals always bragged about their crimes, allowing the hero to escape. The windscreen wipers moved rhythmically like metronomes.

They left Moreton-in-Marsh behind and out they went along the Fosse Way, the Roman road which, like all Roman roads, went straight up hills and down the other side. Roman armies had not gone in for easy detours.

'Right here!' barked Guy.

'This goes to Toddenham,' said Agatha. 'We could have gone round the back of Budgen's.'

'Drive!'

Would Doris Simpson look after her cats? He surely meant to kill them.

'Stop!' he commanded.

Agatha stopped with a squeal of brakes. 'You first,' Guy said to Mrs Bloxby. 'If you run for it, I'll kill her.'

'Run for it,' Agatha urged the vicar's wife. 'He's going to kill both of us anyway.'

But Mrs Bloxby got out and stood meekly beside the car.

'Into the field,' said Guy.

Agatha found she was still clutching her handbag.

As she ducked under the fence, she released the flap and groped for that little can of lacquer.

'Now stand there, together.' The rain had stopped and faint starlight shone on the black revolver in Guy's hand.

He levelled the pistol at them.

Mrs Bloxby left Agatha's side and walked forward and put a hand on his arm.

'This will not do,' she said gently. 'You cannot get away with this.'

He jerked his arm away.

Agatha darted forward and sprayed lacquer in his face. He shouted, clutched at his eyes and dropped the revolver.

The vicar's wife grabbed the revolver and shouted, 'Stand back, Agatha.'

Guy looked at them blearily. 'So go on and shoot.' He advanced on Mrs Bloxby. 'But you won't, will you, oh lady of God? You can't!'

His hand reached out.

Mrs Bloxby shot him full in the chest.

He stared at her in surprise and then down at the spreading stain on his white shirt. 'I'll be damned,' said Guy Freemont.

Mrs Bloxby sat down suddenly on the wet grass. 'Probably,' she said faintly and then buried her face in her hands.

Guy toppled forward on his face and lay still. The moon swam out from behind ragged black clouds. Far away the thunder grumbled.

Agatha walked on shaking legs and pulled Mrs Bloxby to her feet. 'We need to get help and I'm not leaving you here.'

'God forgive me,' whispered Mrs Bloxby. 'I've killed him.'

'Maybe not,' said Agatha. 'But we're not waiting to see.'

She helped the vicar's wife into the car. The keys were still in the ignition. Agatha found that her legs were trembling so much that she could barely press the accelerator.

But she managed to start the car and drive into Toddenham, stopping at the first house.

The householder who answered the door looked at the two women and then down at the gun which Mr Bloxby was still holding in her hands, screamed and slammed the door.

'Give me the gun.' Agatha put it in her handbag.

They walked next door. A slim young man answered it and after listening to their pleas to use the phone, that they had to call the police, invited them in. Agatha called for the police and ambulance, breaking off to ask the young man his address.

'We'd best go back,' said Agatha. 'You wait here, Mrs Bloxby, and I'll stop them.'

'No, I'll come with you. I killed him.'

The young man who had given his name as Gabriel Law made a move to accompany them and then decided against it. If one of these women had killed someone, he felt it would be safer to stay behind.

Agatha drove the short distance to the field. They both sat silently in the car.

'I had to do it,' said Mrs Bloxby at last.

'Yes, you did, or we'd both be dead. How blind I've been! You know how I got on to him?'

'No.'

'Bill Wong said there was a single white Persian cat hair in the turn-up of old Mr Struthers's trousers. But no one could find a trace of a white cat. That was, until just before he arrived at my house this evening. I had been over to see his secretary, Portia Salmond. She said she was having an affair with him. I noticed my blouse, the one I had been wearing when I went to see her – it had white cat hairs on it. Like a fool I first thought that Portia had been the murderer.'

'You would have thought Portia would have got rid of the cat.'

'But no one thought of her. And the police were asking around Ancombe for white cats but they didn't explain why or make the information public. But you knew it was him. Why?'

'The atmosphere of evil when I walked into your sitting-room was almost tangible. And you looked so white and frightened. I put your life at risk, Agatha. I was frightened, too, and that's how I let him know he was suspected. What a silly fool I was. Listen! Is that a police siren?'

Agatha rolled down the window. 'Several,' she said.

They both got out and stood in the road.

Bill Wong erupted out the first car, shouting, 'Where is he?'

'That field, just there.' Agatha pointed.

Bill and Detective Inspector Wilkes and several policemen went into the field. 'Get the ambulance here,' shouted Bill.

Police cars moved to one side to allow the ambulance through.

Agatha and Mrs Bloxby waited and waited. Finally a stretcher with Guy's body on it was gently lifted over the fence. He had an oxygen mask over his face and a drip in his arm.

'He's still alive,' said Mrs Bloxby.

And she began to cry.

Chapter Ten

'So he'll survive after all.' Agatha was talking to Bill Wong in her kitchen a few days after Guy Freemont had been arrested.

'Minus one lung, yes.'

'I'm glad for Mrs Bloxby's sake. I do not know how that good woman would actually have coped with killing someone. Has he confessed yet?'

'He did when he came round after an emergency operation. He thought he was dying, you see. Now he's found out he's not, he's got a lawyer preparing a defence that he was in shock.'

'He won't get away with that!'

'No. He had keys to Portia's house and that's where he killed Struthers. She was out and he phoned Mr Struthers and asked him to come over. When he found out Mr Struthers planned to oppose the water company, he struck him with the poker. He also had the keys to Portia's car, so he bundled Robert in the boot, took him to the spring and dumped him. To make sure Robert was really dead he gave him another blow on the head, hence the blood you saw.'

'Surely Portia isn't completely innocent? Where was she when he was using her car?'

'She was having dinner in a restaurant within walking distance and there are witnesses to that fact.'

'And what about Robina?'

'Portia was helpful there as well,' said Bill. 'She confessed that Guy had met Robina in a pub a week before the fête, but made Portia promise not to tell anyone about it. Back to Guy's confession. Robina was in a state. She said she was sure there must be a loophole in the legal agreement. Guy said there wasn't, and Robina then said she would make a public declaration about her change of mind on the day of the fête and that she had already prepared notes for a speech.

'So Guy nipped away from the fête. He had already typed out notes on an old typewriter which he then dumped in the river. He was standing at the wall when he struck her down, picked up her notes and substituted his own.'

'All that guff he gave me about murder being a useful advertisement was all a lie?' exclaimed Agatha.

'Not quite. He said it had been very useful. His lawyer, of course, is trying to say that because of shock and drugs, he didn't know what he was saying. He won't get away with it. The forensic department took apart Portia's house and found traces of blood on the carpet.'

'Where did she keep the cat?' asked Agatha. 'I didn't see one.'

'After the first murder, she had delivered the cat to her mother's. Said she was too busy to take care of it.'

Agatha scowled horribly. 'I don't think she can be innocent. You didn't broadcast that you were looking for a white cat, but Guy must have known you were looking.'

'It's going to be very hard to prove.'

'And what of brother Peter?'

'He seems to be in the clear. But I don't think the water company will last much longer. Any profit they made will be swallowed up in Guy's defence.'

'Wait a bit,' said Agatha. 'Who wrote those threatening letters?'

'A frightened mad old man from Ancombe. He wandered into the police station to confess. His name is Joe Parr and he has a long history of mental instability.'

'He caused Robina's death,' said Agatha crossly. 'If he hadn't frightened her, then she wouldn't have changed her mind.'

Bill looked at her sympathetically. 'Are you over your shock?'

'I think I'm all right.' Agatha thought back to that terrible evening, of how James had appeared in the light of the police cars, just watching, making no move to come forward and comfort her. 'Mrs Bloxby and I have talked it to death. The fact that she didn't actually kill Guy has done wonders for her. She still feels guilty about nearly getting me killed, you know, giving Guy that lecture about Judgement Day.'

'She was remarkably brave and so were you, Agatha.'

'I was very silly. I hated those insulting bastards on the parish council so much, I was sure it was one of them. Did . . . did Guy say anything about me?'

Bill folded his hands and looked down at them. Guy had actually confessed to romancing Agatha because he had found out her reputation of being an amateur detective and wanted to make sure she didn't suspect him. 'No,' he lied. 'Not a word.'

'I feel such a fool,' mourned Agatha. 'To James it all seemed so obvious that it must have been one of the Freemont brothers, or both.'

'Yes, he dug up some useful information about them. I told you about that.'

'But why didn't he drop me a hint? Why didn't he tell me why he was going up to London?'

'Would you have believed him?'

Agatha coloured. 'Probably not.'

260

'Have you see him?'

'No, only glimpses at police headquarters. He hasn't phoned me and I haven't phoned him. Heard from Sharon?'

'She's walking out with a copper. Seems very happy.'

He probably doesn't live with his parents, thought Agatha.

'Did James ever go out with Portia?' she asked. 'He invited her out.'

'No, I gather he never did.'

'The thing that puzzles me,' said Agatha, 'is that if Mary Owen and her sister were innocent, why did she go to such lengths to frighten me?'

'She's a nasty bully. I almost wish it could have turned out to be her.'

There was a ring at the doorbell. Agatha went to answer it. Roy Silver stood on the doorstep. 'Thought I'd drop down to see you,' he said cheerfully.

'Come in; Bill's here.'

'Bill's just going,' said Bill Wong, appearing behind Agatha. 'I'll see you later.'

'Come in, Roy,' said Agatha. 'What really brings you?'

'Came to offer a shoulder to weep on,' said Roy. 'Read all about it in the newspapers.'

'I'm over the worst of it,' said Agatha. 'How long do you mean to stay?'

'Just for the day. Now tell me all about it.'

They sat over cups of coffee in the kitchen while Agatha told him a highly embroidered account about how she had begun to suspect Guy but had just been stringing him along.

'Fancy some lunch?' said Agatha at last.

'On me, Aggie. Let's nip over to that pub in Ancombe and find out how the locals are taking the news.'

They drove to Ancombe. Leaves from the trees swirled down in front of them and the flowers were turning black with autumn frosts.

'I think I'll take myself abroad somewhere for part of the winter,' said Agatha. 'Can't bear the cold and fogs.'

'Oh, I'd stick around. What about moving up to London?'

'Why?' demanded Agatha suspiciously.

'Just a thought.'

They were settled at a corner table in the pub when the whole of Ancombe Parish Council came in. It transpired that Andy Stiggs had just been made chairman. They made a jolly group.

'You'd never think they hated each other,' marvelled Agatha.

They all saw Agatha, but not one of them came over to say hello. They drank and toasted each other, their voices almost defiant with bonhomie.

'Let's get out of here,' said Agatha when they had finished a not very appetizing lunch.

'The very sight of that lot depresses me. I was so sure it was one of them.'

'I thought you suspected Guy.'

'Not at the beginning,' said Agatha quickly.

When they arrived back at her cottage, James was working in his front garden. He came along to meet them.

'How are you getting along?' James asked Agatha.

'I'm all right now,' said Agatha, fumbling for her house key. 'I could have done with a friend right after it happened.'

'Well, you know,' said James easily, 'I was really cross with you. You were a very silly woman. I told you it was Guy Freemont. But would you listen to me? No. He was obviously only having an affair with you so that you wouldn't suspect him.'

Agatha found her key and unlocked the door. 'Do you mind, James?' she said frostily. 'We're busy.'

He shrugged and turned and strode away.

Roy followed Agatha in. 'It's time you found someone who valued you,' he said.

'Okay.' Agatha heaved a sigh. She suddenly just wanted to be alone. 'When's your train?'

'I thought I'd get the four-fifteen.'

'I'll run you to the station.'

'You know, Agatha, you're wasting your talents. Pedmans has a new account.'

Roy worked for Pedmans. 'Oh, yes?' Agatha's

voice was thin and suspicious but Roy ploughed on regardless.

'It's this soft drink called Healthbuzz, and the boss said you would be the very one to handle it. Where are you going?'

'I am going to phone for a taxi for you,' said Agatha. 'You didn't come here to offer me any comfort. You came here because your boss ordered you to!'

She went and phoned for a taxi.

Roy left, still protesting that he had really only come out of friendship.

The phone rang a few minutes afterwards. It was James. 'Look, Agatha,' he said, 'it's silly, quarrelling like this. Why don't we meet for dinner?'

'All right.'

'I'll pick you up at eight.'

Agatha sat down on a little chair by the phone and put her head in her hands. Why did she not feel either happy or excited?

The phone rang again, making her jump.

'Charles here,' said an upper-class voice. Baronet, Sir Charles Fraith.

'Oh, Charles. How nice to hear from you,' said Agatha.

'I've been on my travels. What about a spot of dinner tonight?'

Agatha opened her mouth to say she couldn't make it and then her face hardened and she found herself saying, 'That would be nice.'

'Where shall we meet?'

'You will come here at eight o'clock and pick me up, Charles,' said Agatha firmly, 'and when the bill for dinner is presented, you will not disappear to the Gents or say you forgot your wallet.'

'You know me of old,' laughed Charles. 'See you at eight.'

Agatha rang off and then phoned James. 'I'm sorry I can't see you this evening,' she said curtly. 'I had forgotten, I have another arrangement. Goodbye, James.' She firmly replaced the receiver.

So another dinner with someone younger, she thought, wearily dragging up the stairs to slap on anti-wrinkle cream.

James Laccy took up a position at the window of his cottage which overlooked the entrance to Agatha's. At eight o'clock, he saw Sir Charles Fraith arrive.

Well, that's that, he thought bitterly. He had planned to explain to Agatha over dinner that he was tired of their quarrels and that he wanted them to get back together again.

But she didn't deserve him, flirting around like a tart!

The fact that Agatha Raisin did not have telepathic powers never crossed his mind.

If you enjoyed *The Wellspring of Death*, read on for the first chapter of the next book in the *Agatha Raisin* series …

Agatha Raisin

AND THE

WIZARD

OF

EVESHAM

Chapter One

The weather was tropical. And this was England and this was Evesham in the Cotswolds. Agatha Raisin drove into the car park at Merstow Green, turned off the air-conditioning, switched off the engine and braced herself to meet the wall of soupy heat which she knew would greet her the minute she stepped out of the car.

Like many, she had decided that all the scares about the greenhouse effect were simply lies made up by eco-terrorists. But this August had seen clammy, sweaty days followed by monsoon thunderstorms at night. Most odd.

Agatha groaned as she left her car and walked across to the parking-ticket machine. What a hell of a day to decide to get one's hair tinted!

She returned to her car and pasted the ticket on the window and then bent down and squinted at herself in the driving-mirror. Her hair was still dark brown but now streaked with purple.

Agatha had gone into a mild depression following her 'last case'. Mrs Agatha Raisin fancied herself to be a detective to rival the fictional ones like Poirot and Lord Peter Wimsey. She was a stocky middle-aged woman with good legs, a round face and small bearlike eyes which looked suspiciously out at the world. Her hair had always been her pride, thick and brown and glossy.

But only that week she had discovered grey hairs, nasty grey hairs appearing all over. She had bought one of those colour rinses but it had turned the grey purple. 'Go to Mr John,' advised Mrs Bloxby, the vicar's wife. 'His place is in the High Street in Evesham. He's supposed to be very good. They say he's a wizard at tinting hair.'

So Agatha had made the appointment and here she was in Evesham, a town situated some ten miles from her home village of Carsely.

The cynics say Evesham is famous for dole and asparagus. Situated beside the river Avon in the Vale of Evesham, the Garden of England, well-known for its nurseries, orchards and, of course, asparagus, Evesham nonetheless can present itself to the visitor who comes to see its historical buildings as a down-at-heel town. Despite the increasing population, shops keep closing up and the boards over the windows are decorated with old Evesham scenes by local artists, so that sometimes it seems a town of pictures and thrift shops. Enormous fecund women trundle push-chairs with small children. The fashion they favour is leggings topped by a baggy blouse. As columnist and TV celebrity Anne Robinson said, she thought leggings came along with push-chairs and babies.

Agatha sometimes thought that a lot of the clothes shops closed down because the buyers would not look out of the window at the size of the female population and stocked only up to size sixteen instead of up to size twenty-two.

She walked over to the High Street, not even stopping to look at the magnificent bulk of the old churches. Agatha was not interested in history as James Lacey, the love of her life, her neighbour, was off once more on his travels, leaving his cottage deserted and Agatha depressed and with grey hairs on her head.

The hairdresser's was simply called Mr John. Mrs Bloxby had urged Agatha to make sure she got Mr John in person.

And there it was, glittering in the heat of the High Street, a discreet shop frontage with mr john emblazoned in curly brass letters over the door.

Agatha pushed open the door and went in. No air-conditioning, of course. This was Britain and there were too many recent memories of cold summers for shopkeepers to decide to put in air-conditioning.

A receptionist marked off Agatha's name in the book and called to a thin, pimply girl to escort Agatha to the salon. Agatha began to wish she had not come. She trudged through to a room at the back and the girl said she would fetch Mr John.

Agatha gazed sullenly at her reflection in the mirror. She felt old and frumpy.

Then suddenly behind her in the mirror, a vision appeared and a pleasant voice said, 'Good afternoon, Mrs Raisin. I'm Mr John.'

Agatha blinked. Mr John was tall and very, very handsome. He had thick blond hair and very bright blue eyes, startlingly blue, as blue as a kingfisher's wing. His face was lightly tanned.

'Now what have we here?' he said.

'We have purple hair,' snapped Agatha, feeling diminished in front of this handsome vision.

'It's easily remedied. Would you also like me to style your hair?'

Agatha, who usually kept her hair short, had let it grow quite long. She shrugged. In for a penny, in for a pound. 'Why not?'

'You're not local, are you?' Mr John stirred the hair tint with strong, well-manicured hands.

'No, I'm from London.' Agatha had no intention of telling Mr John or anyone about her childhood background in a Birmingham slum. 'I had my own public relations business and sold up and took early retirement and moved to Carsely.'

'Pretty village.'

'Yes, very pleasant.'

'And does your husband like it?'

'My husband is dead.'

His hands hovered above her head. 'Raisin. Raisin? That name rings a bell.'

'It should do. He was murdered.'

'Ah, yes, I remember. How terrible for you.'

'I'm over it now. I hadn't seen him in years anyway.'

'Well, an attractive lady like yourself won't remain single for long.'

'I am sure you mean well and that's what you say to all your dreary customers,' said Agatha tetchily, 'but I am well aware of what I look like.'

'Ah, but I haven't done your hair before. By the time I've finished with you, you'll be fighting them off with clubs.'

Agatha suddenly laughed. 'You're very sure of your skill.'

'I have every reason to be.'

'So if you're that good, why Evesham?'

'Why not? I like Evesham. The people are nice. I am king here. I might be lost among the competition in London. There you are. Now, I'll set the timer. Sharon, a coffee and some magazines for Mrs Raisin.'

A woman had entered and was sitting in the chair alongside Agatha. 'Ready to have your colour done again, Maggie?' Mr John greeted her.

'If you think so,' said Maggie, gazing up at him with adoring eyes.

'Did your husband like the new style?'

'He doesn't like anything about me.' Maggie's voice had taken on a querulous moan. 'Insults from morning to night. I tell you, John, if it weren't for you bucking me up, I'd kill myself.'

'There, now. You'll feel better when I've finished with you.'

As Agatha waited for the tint to take effect and more customers were dealt with, some by a couple of assistants, Agatha was amazed at the personal revelations that were poured into the hairdressers' ears.

She covertly watched Mr John as he moved about, admiring his athletic body and his blond hair, and oh, those blue, blue eyes.

Agatha began to feel alive for the first time in weeks.

The timer rang and she was escorted through to a hand-basin and the tint was washed out. Then back to Mr John, who began to put her hair up in rollers.

'I thought it would be a blow-dry.'

'I'm going to put your hair up . . . Agatha. It is Agatha, isn't it?'

A less glorious-looking hairdresser would have been told sharply that it was Mrs Raisin. Agatha nodded.

'You'll love it.'

'I've never had my hair up before. I've always had it short.'

He clicked his tongue. 'Ladies who don't think as much of themselves as they should, always get their hair cut short. Show me a woman with her hair cut to the bone and I'll show you an example of really low self-worth. Tell you what, if you don't like it, I'll take it down again and cut it.'

Agatha reluctantly gave her approval although she could feel sweat trickling down her body. How did Mr John keep so cool?

She was just beginning to feel she had been under the hot drier for hours when she was rescued and taken back to Mr John.

As he worked busily away, Agatha looked in delight as her new appearance emerged. Her hair was glossy and brown once more, but swept up in a French pleat and then arranged around her square face in a way that made it looked thinner. She forgot about the heat. She smiled up at Mr John in sheer gratitude.

It was only when she was walking back down the High Street, squinting in shop windows to admire her reflection, that she realized she had not made another appointment. But Agatha had mostly done her own hair, getting it cut in London on her occasional visits.

Once home, she opened all the doors and windows to try to let in some fresh air. Her two cats darted out into the garden and then promptly lay down on the grass, lethargic in the sun.

She looked at her silent phone. To add to her depression, it never seemed to ring. Her friend, Detective Sergeant Bill Wong was on holiday; Sir Charles Fraith, with whom she had been involved on a couple of cases, was abroad somewhere; James Lacey was God only knew where; and even Roy Silver, her former employee, had not troubled to ring.

Then she remembered there was to be a meeting of the Carsely Ladies' Society that evening. A good opportunity to show off her new hair-style.

Mrs Bloxby was hosting the society at the vicarage and because of the heat had set out chairs and tables in the vicarage garden.

Agatha's hair-style was much admired. 'Where did you go?' asked Mrs Friendly, a plump, cheerful woman who usually lived up to her name. She was a relative newcomer to the village and hailed as an antidote to that other relative newcomer, Mrs Darry, who was nibbling a piece of cake with rabbitlike concentration.

'Mr John in Evesham,' said Agatha.

To her surprise, Mrs Friendly's face creased up like that of a hurt baby. 'I wouldn't go there,' she said, lowering her voice to a whisper.

'Why?' Agatha stared rudely at Mrs Friendly's hair, which was a mousy brown and hanging in damp wisps round her hot face.

'Nothing,' muttered Mrs Friendly. 'One hears stories.'

'About Mr John?'

'Yes.'

'What stories?'

'Must talk to Mrs Bloxby.' Mrs Friendly moved away.

Agatha stared after her and then shrugged. She was joined by Miss Simms, Carsely's unmarried mother and secretary of the society. 'You look drop-dead gorgeous, Mrs Raisin.' Agatha had long ago given up asking other members to call her by her first name. They all seemed to enjoy the old-fashioned formality of second names. Miss Simms was wearing a brief pair of shorts with a halter-top and her usual spiked heels. 'Where did you go?'

'Mr John in Evesham.'

'Oh, I went there once to get my hair done.

I was bridesmaid at my sister Glad's wedding. He did it ever so pretty, but I didn't like him.'

'Why?'

'Awful patronizing, he was. Gushed around the richer customers.'

Agatha shrugged. 'It doesn't really matter what a hairdresser's like, does it?'

'To me it does. I mean to say, I don't like anyone I don't like touching me.'

The meeting was called to order. They were to give one of their concerts over at Ancombe. Agatha's heart sank. Ladies' Society concerts were truly awful, long evenings of shrill singing and bad sketches.

Mrs Darry piped up, her eyes gleaming in her ferrety face. She was wearing a tweed skirt, blouse and tweed jacket but seemed unaffected by the heat. 'Why doesn't Mrs Raisin ever volunteer to do anything?'

'Why don't you?' snapped Agatha.

'Because I am doing the teas.'

'I have no talent,' said Agatha.

Mrs Darry gave a shrill laugh. 'Neither do any of the others, but that doesn't stop them.'

'Really,' protested Mrs Bloxby, 'that was unkind.'

Miss Simms, who had volunteered to do her impersonation of Cher, glared. 'Jealous cow,' she said.

'I've a good mind to let you do the teas yourselves,' said Mrs Darry.

There was a silence. Then Agatha said, 'I'll do it.'

'Good idea,' said Miss Simms.

Mrs Darry got to her feet. 'Then if you don't need my services, I'm going home.'

She stalked out of the garden.

Agatha bit her lip. She didn't want to be bothered catering for a bunch of women in all this heat.

The depression which had lifted because of her visit to the hairdresser came down around her again like a black cloud. This is your life, Agatha Raisin. Trapped in a Cotswold village, cut off from excitement, cut off from adventure, doing teas for a bunch of boring women.

She trudged home afterwards. There did not seem to be a breath of air.

She opened all the windows. She looked at the silent phone. Could anyone have rung when she was out? She dialled 1571 for the Call Minder. 'You have *one* message,' said the carefully elocuted voice of the computer. 'Would you like to hear it?'

'Of course I would, you silly bitch,' growled Agatha.

There was a silence and then the voice said primly, 'I did not hear that. Would you like to hear your message?'

There was a click and then the well-modulated tones of Sir Charles Fraith sounded

279

down the line, 'Hello, Aggie. Fancy dinner tomorrow?'

Agatha brightened. Although she had been wary of Charles because of a one-night stand when they had both been in Cyprus, a night of sex which had seemed to mean very little to him, the thought of going out to dinner and showing off her new hair-style appealed greatly.

She dialled his number and got his Call Minder and left a message asking him to call for her at eight o'clock the following evening.

Her depression once more lifted, she went upstairs and had a bath and went to bed. She had left her hair pinned up, but as she lay on her hot pillow the pins bored into her head. At last she rose and took all the pins out and went back to bed, tossing and turning all night in the suffocating heat. Thunder rolled and the rain came down about two in the morning but did nothing to freshen the air.

When she rose in the morning, it was to find her hair was a disaster, damp with heat, and dishevelled with all the tossing about.

As soon as she knew the salon would be open, she phoned Mr John's receptionist to see if she could have an appointment for that day. 'I am so sorry, Mrs Raisin,' said the receptionist on a rather smug note. 'Mr John is fully booked.'

'Put him on.'

'I beg your parding?'

'I said let me talk to him . . . now!'

'Oh, very well.'

'Agatha!' Mr John welcomed her like an old friend.

'I've got a dinner date and my hair is a wreck. Could you possibly fit me in?'

'I would like to help you out. Let me see. Give me the book, Josie.'

There was a rustling of pages and then he came back on the phone. 'You had your hair washed yesterday, so what I could do is just put it in rollers and then pin it up, but it would need to be five o'clock.'

Agatha thought quickly. She would have plenty of time to get her hair done, get back home and washed and changed in time for Charles. 'Lovely,' she said. 'I'll be there.'

She then went up to the bedroom and swung open the doors of the wardrobe. What to wear? There was that little black dress she hadn't worn since Cyprus. He had liked it. She tried it on. It hung loose on her body. How odd, thought Agatha, that depression could do so effectively what all those diets and exercise had not. She had lost weight.

She decided to drive into Mircester and look for something new.

The steering-wheel of her car scorched her hands and she was up out of the village and speeding along the Fosse before the air-conditioning worked.

Mircester shimmered under ferocious heat. She was able to find a parking place without difficulty. A lot of people seemed to have decided to stay at home. Agatha put on her sunglasses and squinted up at the sky. Not a cloud in sight. She made her way to Harris Street off the main square, which boasted a line of expensive boutiques.

She went in and out of one hot shop after another until she felt she could not bear to try on another dress. Perhaps it would be better to settle for one of her old dresses. It might be a bit loose but that would be all to the good, for any restaurant they went to would not have air-conditioning.

Agatha had just decided to forget about the whole thing when, looking along an alley which led off Harris Street and down to the abbey, she noticed the weekly market was in full swing. She would buy some fresh vegetables for salad. Once she was in the market and heading for the vegetable stalls, she noticed several stalls full of brightly coloured clothes. In one of them, a dress caught her eye. It was of fine scarlet cotton with a design of white lotus flowers. It had a cool, flowing line. Agatha fingered it. An Indian trader appeared at her elbow. 'Nice dress,' he said.

Agatha hesitated and then asked, 'How much?'

'Fourteen pounds.'

Again Agatha hesitated. It was very cheap. It might wrinkle or even fall apart. She had been prepared to spend a couple of hundred pounds. 'Tell you what,' said the trader wearily, 'you can have it for twelve.'

'Okay, I'll take it.'

He stuffed the dress in an old plastic bag.

'Hot, isn't it?' Agatha handed over the money.

'And don't tell me I ought to be used to it,' he said gloomily. 'I was born in Birmingham.'

Agatha was about to say, 'So was I,' but then left the words unsaid. She was ashamed of her background.

She tried on the dress as soon as she got home. It was very attractive and, once she had added a thick gold necklace, looked quite expensive.

Now for Mr John.

Evesham seemed even hotter than Mircester. Agatha suddenly wished she had her old, simple hair-style which she could wash and arrange herself.

But there was Mr John, cool and handsome as ever. 'Got a date?' he asked.

'Yes.'

'Anyone special?'

Agatha could not resist bragging.

'Actually, he's a baronet.'

'Very grand. Which baronet?'

'Sir Charles Fraith.'

'And how did you come to meet him?'

Agatha was about to say, 'On a case,' but she did not like the implication that such as Agatha Raisin could not know anyone with a title, so she said airily, 'He's in my set.'

And hope that shuts you up, she thought.

'Pity,' he said.

'What's a pity?'

'You'll think this very forward of me, but I was thinking of asking you out myself.'

'Why?' asked Agatha in surprise.

'You're a very attractive woman.'

And a rich one, thought Agatha cynically. But then Mr John was so very handsome with his intense blue eyes and blond hair. If James came back and if James saw them going out together, perhaps he would be jealous; perhaps he would be prompted into saying huskily, 'I always loved you, Agatha.'

'Sorry.' Mr John dug a pin into the back of Agatha's hair and her rosy dream burst like a brightly coloured soap bubble.

'Perhaps some evening,' said Agatha cautiously. 'Let me think about it.'

But his invitation gave her a warm little glow, and he was a wizard at fashioning her hair into that elegant style.

Agatha made her way out to her car which she had parked on a double yellow line. 'Look where that car's parked!' hissed a woman at her ear.

Agatha swung round. A dumpy, frumpy woman with thick glasses was glaring at her. Agatha shrugged, walked to her car and opened the door.

'It's yours!' gasped the woman. 'Don't you know it's illegal to park there?'

Agatha turned and faced her. 'I am not obstructing the traffic or getting in anyone's way,' she said evenly. 'Nor am I responsible for the mad parking arrangements of Evesham or for the stupid one-way system. But I wonder where someone like you gets off on this hot day abusing motorists. Go home, have a cup of tea, put your feet up. Get a life!'

And deaf to the insults that began to pour about her ears, Agatha got in and drove off.

Charles arrived promptly at eight o'clock. He gave her a chaste kiss on the cheek. 'Like the hair, Aggie. And the dress. In fact, I bought a dress like that in the market in Mircester this afternoon for my aunt. She was grumbling about not having anything cool to wear.'

'I bought this one in Harrods,' lied Agatha. 'The one in the market must have been a cheap copy.' But her pleasure in her appearance had diminished. 'Where are we eating?'

'I thought we would go to the Little Chef.'

'I am not being taken out to a Little Chef. You *are* cheap, Charles.'

'I like the food,' he said defensively. 'I suppose you want foreign muck. Well, give me a whisky while I think of something.'

Agatha poured him a whisky and he settled in a chair cradling his glass between small, well-manicured hands. He was a slight, fair-haired man. Agatha had never known his age. He had mild, sensitive features and she had originally thought he might be only in his late thirties. But she had later decided he was probably in his mid-forties. He was wearing a shirt open at the neck and had slung his jacket over a chair.

'I know,' he said. 'The Jolly Roger at Ancombe, that new pub.'

'I haven't been there and I don't like the sound of it.'

'Friend of mine went the other week. Said the food was good. Besides, they've got a garden with tables. By the way, I saw that detective friend of yours in Mircester; what's his name, Chinese chap?'

'Bill Wong. But he's on holiday!'

'I suppose he's taking it at home. Had a girl on his arm.'

And he hasn't phoned me, thought Agatha. Bill had been her first friend, the old, tougher Agatha, driven by career and ambition, never having had any time before to make friends.

She could feel the old black edges of that depression hovering on the horizon of her mind.

They set out for Ancombe and parked outside the Jolly Roger, formerly called the Green Man. Inside it was everything that shouted poor food to Agatha – fishing nets, murals of pirates, and waiters and barmen dressed in striped tops and knee-breeches with plastic 'silver' buckles. Charles led the way through to the garden, which was at least a fraction cooler than the inside. A roguish waiter who introduced himself as Henry handed them two large, gaudily coloured menus.

'Oh, shit,' grumbled Agatha. 'Listen to this. Captain Hook's scrumptious potato dip. And what about Barbary Coast Chicken with sizzling Long John corn fritters?'

Henry the waiter was hovering. 'Do you remember when they were called hens, and chickens were the fluffy little yellow things?' asked Agatha.

'And now all mutton is lamb, dear,' said Henry with a giggle.

Agatha eyed him with disfavour. 'Just shove off and stop twitching and grinning and we'll call you when we're ready.'

'Well, *really*, I never did.' Henry tossed his head.

'The fact that you haven't lost your virginity is nothing to do with me. Go away.'

'You've hurt his feelings, Aggie,' said Charles equably.

'Don't care,' muttered Agatha. Bill hadn't even bothered to phone her. 'What are you having?'

'I'll have the all-day breakfast. The Dead-Eye Dick Special, and I hope it comes with lots of chips.'

'No starter? Oh well, I'll have a ham salad.'

'They can't have anything described simply as ham salad.'

'It's described as South Sea Roast pig, sliced and on a bed of crunchy salad with Hard Tack croutons.'

'Oh. Wine?'

'Why not?'

Charles signalled to the waiter, ordered their meals and a carafe of house wine.

'No vintage for me?' asked Agatha.

'I wouldn't bother in a place like this.'

'So why did you bring me to a place like this?'

'God, you're sour this evening, Agatha. Am I to assume that James is not around?'

'No, he's away somewhere.'

'And didn't even say goodbye? Yes, I can see by the look on your face.'

'Men are so immature.'

'That's what you women always throw at us.'

'Well, it's true.'

'It's a necessary part of the masculine make-up. It enables us to dream greater dreams and bring them about. Have you ever wondered why all the great inventors are men?'

'Because women never had a chance.'

'Wrong. Women are pragmatic. They have to be to bring up children. I shall illustrate what I mean with a story.' He rested his chin on his hands and gazed dreamily across at her.

'A chap goes to Cambridge University. The girls there terrify him and they're only interested in rugger-buggers anyway and he's the academic type. So he falls in love with a fluffy little barmaid, and gets her pregnant and marries her. He gets a first in physics but he has to support his new family, so he takes a job in an insurance office and there he is, up to his neck in a mortgage and car payments and the wife has twins. A few years pass and he begins to spend every weekend down in the garden shed. Wife begins to whine and complain. "We never see you. Sharon and Tracey are missing their dad. What are you *doing*?" At last he tells her. He's building a time machine. Then the shit hits the fan. Will this pay the bills? she rages at him. The Joneses next door have a new deep freeze. When are they going to get one? And so on. So he locks himself into his shed and hammers away while she screams outside.

'Well, he builds his time machine and becomes a billionaire and runs off with a little bit of fluff in the office who is the only woman who really understands him and has supported him, which of course she has, not knowing one word he's been talking about, but likes the excitement of being involved with a married man. He divorces his wife and marries the office girl and the money goes to her head and she joins the Eurotrash and runs off with a racing driver and they all live unhappily ever after. And the moral of that is, men and women are different and should start to accept the differences.'

Agatha laughed. 'Couldn't he have escaped in his time machine?'

'Of course not. He got billions to destroy it. Can't have people zipping around the centuries and messing up history.'

'I never know if you're a male chauvinist oink or just being funny.'

'I'm never funny. Look at the wrinkles on my forehead, Aggie. Product of deep thought. So what about you? No nice juicy murders?'

'Nothing at all. I am yesterday's sleuth.'

'I should have thought your experiences in Cyprus would have given you enough death and mayhem for life.'

Cyprus. Where she had passed a night with Charles and James had found out about it and things had never been the same again. Agatha would not admit to herself that her relationship with James had been on the rocks for a long time before that.

Charles watched the shadow fall across her eyes and said gently. 'It wouldn't have worked, you know. James is a twenty-per-cent person.'

'I don't understand you.'

'It's like this. You are an eighty-five-per-cent person and James only gives twenty per cent. It's not a case of won't, it's a case of can't. A lot of men are like that but women will never understand. They go on giving. And they think if they go to bed with the twenty-per-center, and they give that last fifteen per cent, they'll miraculously wake up next to a hundred-per-center. Wrong. If they wake up next to him anyway, it'll be a miracle. Probably find a note on the pillow saying, "Gone home to feed the dog," or something like that.'

Agatha remembered nights with James and mornings when he was always up first, when he never referred to the night before or hugged her or kissed her.

'Maybe I was just the wrong woman,' she conceded.

'Trust me, dearest. Any woman is the wrong woman for James.'

'Perhaps I would have been happy to settle for twenty per cent.'

'Liar. Here's our food.'

To Agatha's surprise, the ham was delicious and the salad fresh and crisp.

'So we're never to go detecting again?' Charles asked, pouring ketchup on his chips.

'I can't go around finding bodies to brighten up my life.'

'No more public relations work?'

'None. All my efforts are going towards providing tea and cakes for the ladies of Ancombe.'

'You'll stir something up, Aggie. No new men on the horizon?'

'One very gorgeous man.'

'Who?'

'My hairdresser.'

'Ah, the one that's responsible for the new elegance.'

'Him.'

'Hairdressers are fickle. I remember ... Never mind.'

'What about *your* love life, Charles?'

'Nothing at the moment.'

They passed the meal reminiscing about their adventures in Cyprus and then he drove her home.

'Am I going to stay the night?' asked Charles as they stood together on Agatha's doorstep.

'No, Charles, I'm not into casual sex.'

'Who says it would be casual?'

'Charles, you demonstrated in Cyprus that I am nothing more than a temporary amuse-

292

ment to you. Has it ever dawned on you that you might be a twenty-per-center yourself?'

'Ouch! But think on this, Aggie. Any eighty-five-per-center who hangs around with twenty-per-centers is just as afraid of commitment.'

He waved to her and went off to his car.

Agatha let herself in, feeling flat. No messages on the phone for her. And what had Bill Wong been thinking of not to phone her?

The sensible thing would be to phone him, and yet Agatha dreaded the idea of finding out she had lost the affection of her first friend.

Life went on. She had to keep moving. Perhaps she would accept Mr John's invitation after all.

Penelope Keith stars as Agatha Raisin in these
full-cast BBC Radio 4 dramas

To order your copies of other books in the Agatha Raisin series simply contact The Book Service (TBS) by phone, email or by post. Alternatively visit our website at www.constablerobinson.com.

No. of copies	Title	RRP	Total
	Agatha Raisin and the Quiche of Death	£6.99	
	Agatha Raisin and the Vicious Vet	£6.99	
	Agatha Raisin and the Potted Gardener	£6.99	
	Agatha Raisin and the Walkers of Dembley	£6.99	
	Agatha Raisin and the Murderous Marriage	£6.99	
	Agatha Raisin and the Terrible Tourist	£6.99	
	Agatha Raisin and the Wellspring of Death	£6.99	
	Agatha Raisin and the Wizard of Evesham	£6.99	
	Agatha Raisin and the Witch of Wyckhadden	£6.99	
	Agatha Raisin and the Fairies of Fryfam	£6.99	
	Agatha Raisin and the Love from Hell	£6.99	
	Agatha Raisin and the Day the Floods Came	£6.99	
	Agatha Raisin and the Curious Curate	£6.99	
	Agatha Raisin and the Haunted House	£6.99	
	Agatha Raisin and the Deadly Dance	£6.99	
	Agatha Raisin and the Perfect Paragon	£6.99	
	Agatha Raisin and Love, Lies and Liquor	£6.99	
	Agatha Raisin and Kissing Christmas Goodbye	£6.99	
	Agatha Raisin and a Spoonful of Poison	£6.99	
	Agatha Raisin: There Goes the Bride (hardback)	£14.99	

And available in 2010 …

No. of copies	Title	Release date	RRP	Total
	Agatha Raisin: There Goes the Bride	April 2010 (paperback)	£6.99	
	Agatha Raisin and the Busy Body	Oct 2010	£14.99	
	Grand total			£

FREEPOST RLUL-SJGC-SGKJ, Cash Sales Direct Mail Dept., The Book Service, Colchester Road, Frating, Colchester, CO7 7DW. Tel: +44 (0) 1206 255 800.
Fax: +44 (0) 1206 255 930. Email: sales@tbs-ltd.co.uk

UK customers: please allow £1.00 p&p for the first book, plus 50p for the second, and an additional 30p for each book thereafter, up to a maximum charge of £3.00. Overseas customers (incl. Ireland): please allow £2.00 p&p for the first book, plus £1.00 for the second, plus 50p for each additional book.

NAME (block letters): _____

ADDRESS: _____

_____

_____ POSTCODE: _____

I enclose a cheque/PO (payable to 'TBS Direct') for the amount of

£_____

I wish to pay by Switch/Credit Card

Card number: _____

Expiry date: _____ Switch issue number: _____